UPSIDE DOWN MAGIC

STICKS AND STONES

Scholastic Children's Books
An imprint of Scholastic Ltd
Euston House, 24 Eversholt Street,
London, NW1 1DB, UK
Registered office: Westfield Road, Southam,
Warwickshire, CV47 0RA

First published in the US by Scholastic Inc, 2016
First published in the UK by Scholastic Ltd, 2016
This edition published in the UK by Scholastic Ltd, 2019

Text copyright © Sarah Mlynowski, Lauren Myracle and
Emily Jenkins, 2016

The right of Sarah Mlynowski, Lauren Myracle and Emily Jenkins to
be identified as the authors of this work has been asserted by them.
ISBN 978 1407 19184 3

Printed by CPI Group (UK) Ltd, Croydon, CR0 4YY
Papers used by Scholastic Children's Books are made from wood
grown in sustainable forests.

1 3 5 7 9 10 8 6 4 2

www.scholastic.co.uk

UPSIDE DOWN MAGIC

STICKS AND STONES

Sarah Mlynowski ★ Lauren Myracle ★ Emily Jenkins

For our Fuzzies: Al, Jamie, Ivy, Maya, Mirabelle, Alisha, Hazel, Chloe, and Anabelle. Treats and hugs forever. (And yes, of course you can each get a unicorn for your birthday!)

1

When Nory Horace turned into a koat, she had
the body of a black kitten and the head of a tiny
goat. She could jump from the floor to the
kitchen counter. She could root through the
laundry and nibble on yummy socks. She was
good at chasing butterflies.

Her koat was a pretty awesome animal, actually, but Nory's aunt Margo didn't like it.

Koat-Nory ate Aunt Margo's flowers.

And her carpets.

And, of course, her socks.

Yesterday morning, Koat-Nory ate all the

Fruity Doodles breakfast cereal, plus the box it came in.

Plus the tablecloth, two loaves of bread, and a part of Aunt Margo's couch.

Nory was a Fluxer. Her magic talent was that she could change into animals. But most Fluxers transformed into ordinary creatures like cats and dogs and rabbits. Nory was different. She *could* become ordinary animals . . . but they didn't stay ordinary for very long.

Aunt Margo had specifically asked Nory not to flux into a koat today, because Margo's boyfriend, Figs, was coming over for dinner and Margo wanted the place to stay clean. Also, kids weren't supposed to do magic without supervision until they grew up and got licensed. (As if anyone followed *that* rule.)

Nory loved Aunt Margo and didn't want to let her down. She planned to stay in plain old girl form. Brown skin, bright eyes, big hair, lucky

6

purple jeans, new red sneakers.

Aunt Margo had left early for her taxi job, so Nory was alone. She was standing on the porch of Margo's small clapboard house in the town of Dunwiddle, waiting for her friend Elliott. She figured this way, even if she did flux into a koat by accident, the house would stay clean.

Nory and Elliott usually walked to school together.

But today turned out to be different. Today, Elliott was late.

Nory noticed a butterfly flapping overhead and wondered if she could change into a koat really quickly and then change back. It felt so *good* to chase a butterfly as a koat.

No, no, no, Nory told herself. *No koat this morning. No unsupervised fluxing.*

The butterfly fluttered above her face.

No, no, no koat! Don't flux!

As with most people, Nory's magic had bubbled up when she was ten. Before that, she'd gone to ordinary school, as everyone else did. Starting in fifth grade, kids went to magic school.

Her new school, Dunwiddle, was a public magic school. That meant anyone could go there, unlike the private academies, which were expensive and hard to get into. Dunwiddle offered classes like math and literature and gym, as well as standard magic classes for the five categories of regular magic students—Flyers, Flares, Fluxers, Fuzzies, and Flickers. Flyers flew. Flares had fire magic. Fluxers turned into animals. Fuzzies could communicate with animals. Flickers could become invisible or turn other things invisible.

But not every kid had regular magic. Nory didn't, for example. So there was a problem for schools: Where should they put the students whose magic was unusual?

As an answer, Dunwiddle had started offering a new class. It was called Upside-Down

Magic. Nory's father had sent Nory to live with her aunt just so she could be in it. There were seven other fifth-grade kids in the class. Like Nory, all of them had something wonky about their talent. Only they weren't supposed to say *wonky*. Their teacher, Ms. Starr, wanted everyone to say *different* or *unusual* instead.

Nory wished the kids in the regular classes would follow that rule, but most of them didn't. Lots of them called the UDM kids wonky. Or they called them Flops. A group of fifth-grade Flares were the worst. They called themselves the Sparkies, and they teased the UDM kids as much as possible. "Look, there's that wonko who turned into a skunkephant and smelled up the whole cafeteria," they told anyone who would listen.

(And, yes, Nory *had* turned into a skunk-elephant earlier in the year. She *had* smelled up the whole cafeteria. But did the Sparkies need to rub it in? *No*.)

Nory bounced on her toes. She turned her head from right to left, searching for Elliott. Instead, she spotted a skinny dark-haired boy skidding around the street corner and running her way. He was flushed and sweaty. He wore a baseball cap and a navy shirt with white lettering that read CIDER CUP POLICE SQUAD. It was Bax Kapoor, another UDM kid.

"You're going to be late!" Bax called as he dashed by.

Yikes. He was right.

"Hey, wait!" Nory called, sprinting after him.

Bax looked over his shoulder but kept going.

Then, *whoa*!

His feet flew up. His head whipped forward, his arms windmilled, and he went down hard.

BAM!

Nory cringed and slapped her hand over her eyes. She peeked through her fingers, already knowing what she would see.

Yep, Bax had turned into a rock.

That was his upside-down magic. Bax was a Fluxer, but he didn't flux into animals. He fluxed into a rock. He did it every day, and pretty much never on purpose. Always he turned into the same enormous gray rock. Well, once he'd fluxed into a leash, but that was an exception. Every other time? Enormous. Gray. Rock.

Nory raced over. "Bax! Are you all right?"

She was met with silence, since Rock-Bax couldn't talk. Also, Rock-Bax couldn't flux back, which made Nory feel really bad for him. It would be dreadful, she thought, to flux into a rock—with no mouth, no arms, no ears—and to be *stuck* like that. For him to change back, somebody had to take him to the nurse's office for an icky green potion that did the trick.

Nory's shoulders sagged. Today, she would have to be that somebody.

They were both going to be *really* late for school.

2

Bax's head hurt. His feet hurt; his arms hurt. Even his earlobes hurt. Why did it hurt so much after he fluxed?

Bax never knew what went on when he was a rock. Other Fluxers kept their human minds when they changed into animal forms. Well, most of the time. Keeping control over your human mind was an important Fluxer technique, but Bax had zero control over anything when he fluxed. He hated it.

Bax remembered running to school, and he remembered tripping. After that, everything was a blank.

Now he found himself in the nurse's office.

"Good morning, good morning," Nurse Riley said, smiling.

Bax blinked and tried to get his bearings. He was sitting on a cot. A scratchy blue blanket was draped over his shoulders, and his tongue felt slimy. It was because of the Burtlebox, the icky green potion Nurse Riley used to turn him back into a boy.

Bax hated Burtlebox. It tasted like rotten lettuce. And how did it end up in his *mouth?* Nurse Riley applied it to Rock-Bax with a paintbrush.

Nurse Riley was cool, though. He had sideburns and an easy grin, and he acted as if it were perfectly normal to paint Bax with green smelly stuff on a daily basis.

"You fluxed on the way to school," Nurse Riley said.

"Who brought me here?"

"Nory Horace. Delivered you in an old-time baby carriage, if you can believe it."

"A *baby carriage?*"

"Wasn't that resourceful? Nory got it from her aunt's garden. Her aunt uses it to hold potted plants."

Bax had been in Nory's backyard. Now he noticed the carriage in the corner of the room. It was just as he remembered it: large and curved, with spindly wheels.

Nory had pushed him to school in it. She'd pushed him to school like a *doll*.

"I might throw up," he said.

Nurse Riley handed him the trash can. "I could get you a Jell-O cup if you'd like. To settle your stomach?"

"That's okay." Bax waited till the nausea passed. Then he stood up. The blue blanket slid off him. "I should go to class."

"Ah, yes, you should," said Nurse Riley. He

clapped Bax on the back. "I'll see you this afternoon, most likely."

Bax moaned.

Nurse Riley put his hand to his heart and staggered back, pretending to be wounded. "I never mind a visit from you, Bax. You're one of my favorite patients."

"It's not you. It's just—I'm turning into a rock more than ever."

"I don't know. You did the leash that one time. And Ms. Starr says you're making good progress. She says your headstands are getting stronger."

"She is crazy about headstands for kids with upside-down magic," said Bax. "Someone should get her a headstand for her birthday."

Nurse Riley laughed.

Bax left the infirmary and walked slowly to class. The halls were lined with bright red fire extinguishers to keep Flare problems in line.

Neatly printed signs were everywhere:

NO FIRES EXCEPT IN THE FLARE LAB.

RECKLESS FLYING PROHIBITED.

FUZZIES MAY NOT BRING MICE, RATS, OR SNAKES

TO SCHOOL WITHOUT WRITTEN PERMISSION.

Bax spotted a couple of new school-spirit posters on the lockers. There were sign-ups for the Dunwiddle kittenball team and other after-school clubs. Fly-ball. Invisible diving.

Bax passed the regular fifth-grade Fluxer class and saw students sitting at their desks, taking notes. Regular Fluxers were expected to master a black kitten within the first month. After that, they worked on adding colors to their kittens: calico, ginger, tabby, and so on.

"Persians are difficult because of their long fur," Bax heard the teacher say. "Long fur requires sustained control, and of course it's hard to keep neat."

Bax paused at the edge of the door. He watched the teacher climb onto a table in her human form.

"Is everyone watching?" She fluxed smoothly into a fluffy white Persian cat with a squished face. Then she fluxed back. "The flattened facial features take practice," she said. "And that leads me to your homework for tonight."

Bax trudged on. He would never be in that class. He would probably never flux into even the simplest black kitten. The other Fluxers would never stop thinking he was weird.

At the far end of the hall was a giant glass collection jar labeled PENNIES FOR POTIONS. It was a school-wide charity drive that had been going on for a week. Kids brought in their spare pennies, and when the jar was full, the school would donate the money to fund potions for a medical clinic in a poor neighborhood. Bax fished in his pockets, but came up empty.

Sheesh. He'd meant to bring pennies, but he'd forgotten.

He promised himself he'd come in a little earlier and bring some tomorrow. There was a big spare-change bowl on the kitchen counter at home, and Bax was sure his dad wouldn't mind him taking a handful of pennies.

When he got to the Upside-Down Magic classroom, he found Ms. Starr swirling a Hula-Hoop around her waist. She wore a hot-pink blouse and matching sneakers.

"You concentrate with your body, not your mind," she said as Bax walked in.

There was a pile of colorful plastic hoops on the carpeted area of the classroom. "Just like headstands," Ms. Starr said, still hooping. "At first, you think. Then you do. But with practice, you begin to do *without* thinking. It's a wonderful way to connect to your own unique magic."

Ms. Starr was always having them do things that seemed strange and silly. Headstands. Interpretive dance. Balancing poses. Deep breathing. Trust exercises. Sharing their feelings.

Secretly, Bax admired her. A lot. But he tried to be cool and not show it.

Ms. Starr waved at Bax to say hello, but didn't interrupt the lesson to ask him where he'd been. Probably because she already knew. Nory had likely told the entire class about how she'd heroically rescued Bax in a baby carriage.

His skin grew hot. How many people had seen him in it?

Bax dropped into his seat and tried to stop thinking about it. He glanced around. Besides him and Nory, there were only four UDM kids in class today.

Andres floated on the ceiling. He was an Upside-Down Flyer.

Sebastian saw invisible things. He was an Upside-Down Flicker.

Pepper frightened animals. She was an Upside-Down Fuzzy.

Marigold shrank things. Nobody knew what Marigold was.

There were two students missing: Elliott, an Upside-Down Flare who made ice, and Willa, an Upside-Down Flare who made it rain indoors.

Ms. Starr talked more about the symbolism of circles. Then she made all the students stand up and get Hula-Hoops. There was room for everyone in the carpeted section of the classroom.

"Hey! Bax!" Nory said in a low voice. "You feeling better?"

Bax pretended he hadn't heard.

"Bax! Can I tell you something?" she persisted.

"We're supposed to be hula-hooping," said Bax.

"I put a towel over you and brought you in the back door of the school."

"You what?"

Nory shrugged. "I would hate it if I fluxed and couldn't change back. And I would hate it even more if someone saw me arriving at school like that. I figured you wouldn't want anyone to see you in the c-a-r-r-i-a-g-e."

"Everyone here can spell *carriage*, Nory."

"Okay, but nobody saw. That's all I wanted to tell you."

Bax knew he should say thank you, but the words wouldn't come. Instead, he said, "You've never gotten stuck. You're always able to flux back after you turn into something."

Nory paused for a second. Then she said, "Did I tell you that once I fluxed into a puppy with squid legs?"

"Ew."

"I smeared squid ink all over my dad's slippers. Then I chewed them. I attached myself to the bathroom wall and squirted ink at my brother, too."

"Nory! Bax!" said Ms. Starr. "Less lips, more hips. Get hooping!"

Both Nory and Bax picked up their hoops, but Bax couldn't focus on his "mind-body connection," or whatever it was Ms. Starr was hoping they'd work on. The only thing on his mind was that he'd pick *puppy with squid legs* over *rock* any day. No contest.

3

Elliott and Willa showed up during math.

"Where were you?" Nory mouthed at Elliott.

"Tutoring," Elliott whispered.

"Again?" Nory waved her hand at her teacher. "Ms. Starr? How come Elliott and Willa get two tutoring sessions before the rest of us even get one?"

The students had been studying upside-down magic skills with Ms. Starr since the start of the school year, but now they were each beginning tutoring for their particular talents, twice a week. Elliott and Willa were paired together because they were both Upside-Down Flares. Sebastian would have a Flicker tutor, since his magic was related to invisibility. Nory and Bax would work together because they were both Fluxers. Andres would have a Flyer tutor, since he couldn't get down from the ceiling. And Pepper would see a Fuzzy tutor, since she had upside-down animal magic.

Ms. Starr answered Nory: "It takes time to organize with the various tutors. The Flare tutor has a very flexible schedule, so Elliott and Willa were able to begin right away." She clapped her hands. "Kids, get out your poetry books. We will begin with the poem about a phoenix on page thirty-eight, and after reading it and discussing, we will do interpretive dance. Except for Nory and Bax." She winked at Nory. "You two are excused now, for tutoring with Mr. Vitomin."

Nory jumped out of her seat. Zamboozle!

She was excused from interpretive dance *and* she had a tutor!

"Have you found anyone for me yet?" Marigold asked.

"Not yet," Ms. Starr answered. "Your shrinking magic is wonderfully different, which makes it tricky to find a tutor who's a good fit. But rest assured, we will."

"Yesterday I shrank my toothbrush while I was brushing my teeth," Marigold said. "I almost swallowed it. I'm worried I'll accidentally shrink a *person* one of these days. Then what would I do?"

"Give him your tiny toothbrush," Andres replied from the ceiling.

Ms. Starr put her hand on Marigold's shoulder. "You have an extraordinary talent, Marigold," she said. "Don't lose faith, okay?"

Nory closed the classroom door behind her. She and Bax went down the hall and up the stairs to the second floor. Mr. Vitomin's office was decorated with sports trophies and pictures of fierce-looking wildcats: lynxes, panthers, and lots of tigers. There was a mini fridge at one end. On the other end, a counter was covered with bags of nuts, dried fruit, and other healthy-looking food. The room smelled like herbal tea.

Mr. Vitomin himself was a short, pale, bald man. He had rosy cheeks and big muscles. The muscles bulged and made the fabric of his T-shirt strain across his chest.

He pointed at Nory and Bax in turn. "Let me get this straight. You're Elinor and you're Box?"

"I go by Nory, and he's *Bax*," Nory said.

"I thought it was *Box*. You a boxer, boy?" Mr. Vitomin bounced around like a prizefighter.

Bax didn't say anything.

"For the love of carrots, speak up, son!" said Mr. Vitomin. "Oh, hey, are you both eating seaweed snacks and protein? Good nutrition is the basis of good fluxing. All my students eat a carrot, two sardines, and a handful of pumpkin seeds before every lesson. And we all drink pomegranate juice and ginger tea." He stuck out his hand. "I'm Mr. Vitomin, but you can call me Coach."

He pumped Nory's hand vigorously, then Bax's.

"I'm the coach of the upper-grade kittenball team, the Dunwiddle Catnips. I think this year we've got the finest group of swatters in the county." He grinned. "We're starting a kittenball club this year, too, for beginners to learn the sport. Can't wait. You watching the game tomorrow night?"

"What game?" asked Nory.

"Tigerball. Professional league. Friday. First game of the season!"

"I'm watching it," mumbled Bax.

Nory didn't know much about tigerball. She had played soccer in ordinary school, before she'd moved in with Aunt Margo. But back when she lived with her father and brother and sister, only her older brother, Hawthorn, ever watched sports.

She did know that tigerball was a team sport, and that high-level Fluxers played it with huge balls of yarn—in tiger form. Kittenball was the kid version.

Mr. Vitomin high-fived Bax. Bax winced.

"Best sport in the world, yeah, son?" Mr. Vitomin said. "Who's your team?"

"San Antonio Stripeys."

"Nah, the Stripeys never take it. It's gonna be the Pouncers all the way this year." Coach rubbed his hands together. "Now, show me what you two can do."

"As Fluxers?" Nory asked.

"Of course!"

"But, Mr. Vitomin—"

"Coach," he corrected.

Nory swallowed. "But, Coach Vitomin—"

"Just Coach. Say it with me: *Coach.*"

"Coach?" Nory said.

"Yes?"

"Didn't Ms. Starr tell you about us? Our magic's upside down."

Coach waved his hand dismissively. "She might have given me your files. I don't know, and it doesn't matter. You're fifth graders, so we'll start with kittens. And I'm tooting my own horn here, but I'm a darn good feline Fluxer. *Darn* good. Do you know how many different house cats I have in my repertoire?"

Nory tried to catch Bax's eye.

"Go on, guess," Coach urged.

"Six?" Nory said.

"Nineteen!" Coach banged on the table and grinned. "Persian, Maine Coon, Siamese, Munchkin, domestic shorthair in twelve colors, Bengal, Burmese, and American Curl."

"Wow," Nory said. But she was thinking, *We can't start with kittens. Bax doesn't do kittens. Bax does rocks. Or rather, just one rock, same rock, every time. Does Coach not understand?*

Coach drew himself up. "Want to see my house cats? All righty, then!"

The air shimmered. Coach Vitomin's muscles bunched and twitched, and . . . *zwoop*! He went through all nineteen breeds of cat, finishing with the black cat that most people learned as a beginner animal.

Then he shifted back to his natural form.

Nory clapped.

Bax did not.

"Now you, Nory," Coach announced. "Let's see your kitten."

Nory *could* do a kitten. A black, beginner kitten, like most fifth-grade Fluxers could. Yes, her magic was upside down, and yes, she often made mixed-up animals like the koat. She could usually hold her kitten shape, though. Usually. She could also keep hold of her human mind while she did it. It had taken a lot of practice, but earlier in the school year, she'd learned.

But it didn't take much for Nory to mess up. She'd add in a goat and become a koat. Or she'd add in a beaver and become a bitten. Or a dragon, and become a dritten.

Now she did what Coach asked. She concentrated. Her heart beat faster. *Pop! Pop! Pop!* Her body stretched and shrank.

Hurrah! She was Kitten-Nory. So far, so good. She swished her tail. She hopped up on the table and licked her paw.

"Very nice," Coach said. He walked around her, examining her from every angle. "You have better whiskers than a lot of first-year Fluxers. And you can hear me? You've got the human mind?"

Nory nodded.

"Well, what's gone wonky, then? Why are you in the upside-down magic class?"

Kitten-Nory looked at him reproachfully. Coach shouldn't say *wonky*. He should say *unusual*.

"You don't want to know," said Bax, sullen.

"Oh, but I do," said Coach. "I'm the tutor! Go on, let's see it, Nory!"

Nory nodded. Then huge, violet dragon wings sprouted from the middle of her spine, and sharp claws curved from her kitten paws. She was a dritten.

She roared, and Coach jumped. She flapped her great wings and flew into the air, circling twice around the small office.

Then she hit the ceiling fan and crashed into the counter. She sent seaweed snacks, bags of nuts, and explosions of protein powder flying across the room.

Oops.

Embarrassed, she popped back into Girl-Nory again. She was sprawled on the floor, covered with almonds.

"Sorry," she said in a small voice.

"That was fan*tas*tic!" cried Coach, helping Nory up. "Ever think about kittenball? With fluxing powers like yours, you'll have a tiger by early high school, I bet! Good for college applications! And that creature you fluxed into: I wonder if it counts as a kitten, what with the wings and the claws and everything."

"It's a dritten," said Nory. "Dragon-kitten."

"Outstanding," Coach murmured. "And it *could* be fair play on the kittenball field." He rested his hand on his chin. "You had the kitten body. You had all four paws. I'll have to look at the rule books."

Nory glowed. Her own father hadn't wanted her at his magic academy. But here was Coach, who knew tons about magic, saying he thought her powers were special. Could she really become a tiger by high school? Or maybe even a dragon-tiger—a driger?

Coach was the best tutor ever.

Coach was the worst tutor ever. He didn't like Bax. Bax could tell.

Well, fine. Bax didn't like Coach, either. Kittenball? Nineteen house cats? Pomegranate juice and ginger tea?!

He wasn't going to be able to help Bax.

He didn't even know Bax's name.

He was going to be tutoring Nory all the time, when Nory barely needed help. Her wonky magic wasn't anywhere near as bad as Bax's was.

Coach loomed over Bax now. Bax backed away.

"Let's see your kitten, Box! Don't be shy. Kitten, and whatever you've got after that!"

Bax stared at the floor.

"Son, wake up!" Coach said. "Show me your kitten."

Bax looked at the floor some more.

"You can do a kitten, can't you?" Coach asked.

Bax shook his head.

"How about a partial kitten? Can you give yourself a tail, say? Some fifth graders start out with just the tail."

"No."

Coach sighed. "Fine. Whatever you do, just show me."

Bax chewed the inside of his cheek. If he turned into a rock, he wouldn't be able to turn himself back. Then he'd have to take the Burtlebox again. He'd had a dose already this morning, not more than two hours ago.

"I'm here to help, for sardine's sake," said Coach. "Don't you *want* help with your upside-down magic?"

Bax did, actually. He hated turning into a rock! He disappeared. He had no way of knowing what happened while he was in rock form.

Where did he go, the part of him that made him Bax?

So *yes*, Bax wanted help. But he didn't think Coach would even know where to start.

"All students can get better at fluxing, but only if they try," Coach said. "Are you willing to try, son?"

"I'm not your son," Bax snapped.

Coach ran his hand over his bald head. He was silent for a full minute. Then he turned to Nory and said to her: "Listen up. Monday is the start of after-school sports, including the beginner kittenball club. In the club, you won't compete, but you'll learn the sport, meet new people, and have a lot of fun. Mondays and Wednesdays. What do you say?"

"I say okay." Nory grinned widely.

Bax just stood there.

He didn't flux into a rock. Yet even so, he'd managed to disappear.

4

Elliott showed up to walk with Nory to school the next morning, Friday, just like normal.

"Where were you yesterday?" Nory asked.

"At school, just like you," Elliott said. "Der. Hey, how'd your first tutoring session go? Is Mr. Vitomin any good?"

"I'm talking about yesterday *morning*," pressed Nory. "I waited for you for six thousand hours."

"For our tutoring session, Willa and I went swimming. Isn't that cool?"

"Yes. But you didn't answer my question."

"We used the high school pool," Elliott continued. "Our tutor's trying a technique called *aquamerge*. We have to connect with the water element, since we're Flares and water's the opposite of fire. Willa made it rain in the pool."

"Elliott."

"Guess what? I think it's meatball day in the cafeteria," said Elliott. "Meatball day is my favorite."

Fine. He wasn't going to tell her.

When they arrived at school, Elliott stepped through the heavy front doors first—"Whoa!" His feet did a crazy dance and he dropped to the floor on his bum. "Ow!"

Nory slipped next. *Bam! Ouch!*

Marigold was several feet in front of them, and she went down, too. Hard. "Marbles!" she said. "Why are there *marbles* everywhere?"

Hordes of kids poured into the building, and nearly everyone hit the floor. Limbs flailed. There were yelps of pain and surprise. It was chaos.

Nory scooched to a safe place against the wall. She drew her knees close and picked up one of the marbles.

Oh. It wasn't a marble, actually. It wasn't made out of glass. It was gray and cool in her hand. A rock.

The hall was really noisy now. Kids in kitten shape batted the stones around the floor. Kids in human shape got up and fell down again. Flyers launched themselves off the floor, but collided with one another and crashed back down.

A sixth-grade girl yelled when a stone rolled off the top of her locker and bonked her on the head. A seventh-grade boy shrieked when his friend dropped a handful of rocks down the back of his pants.

"Enough!" Principal Gonzalez boomed, appearing out of nowhere. The principal was a Flicker. He could do that sort of thing. "Students, get yourselves under control. Fluxers, take human form! Flyers, feet on the ground immediately. Everyone stop moving. I've called the janitor, and she's on her way."

Nory peered through the forest of bodies. Principal Gonzalez tugged at his tie.

"It seems that our Pennies for Potions have been magicked into stones, the whole enormous jar of them," he said. "Eighth graders, if this is a prank, it's not funny."

"It wasn't us!" called an eighth-grade girl.

The principal studied the eighth graders and nodded to himself. "I need to check the other halls. You all stay where you are until we get the stones cleared up. We don't want any injuries."

Then he vanished.

Quietly, and then louder, people began to murmur.

"We had a thousand pennies *at least*! Who's going to give our pennies back?"

"It's got to be an upside-down magic thing."

"The Pennies for Potions jar must have exploded," someone said.

"Do you think those wonko kids can *explode* things?"

"I don't know."

"Can they turn pennies into stones?"

"My mom says they're dangerous."

"It's not their fault—they were born that way."

"It's their fault if they turn our charity money to stone!"

Next to Nory, Marigold pulled herself up on the water fountain. She got slowly to her feet, but her foot slipped again on a rock. Her elbow jammed against the fountain handle. *Swoosh!* Water squirted in a huge spray—and the spray hit Lacey Clench smack in the face.

Lacey Clench was the number-one meanie of the Sparkies. They were the Flare kids who gave the UDM kids such a hard time.

Like most bullies, Lacey was scared and jealous and disappointed. It made her mean. She was also powerful. It wasn't her Flare magic that was powerful. It was her personality. She believed in rules. She was a leader, full of big ideas.

Lacey had flared Elliott's bike tires, melting them to rubber goo. She had set Andres's leash on fire, the leash that kept him from floating into the sky when he was outdoors. She had mocked Bax. She insulted Nory every chance she got.

Lacey and her Sparkie friends, Rune and Zinnia, were bad news.

Now Lacey was soaked in water from the fountain. "You wonko!" she yelled at Marigold. Her thin blond hair was pasted to her skull, and her large round glasses were splattered with droplets. She wailed and wrung out the bottom of her cardigan. "My sweater is ruined!"

"I lost my footing on a rock," said Marigold, touching her hearing aid as if Lacey's yelling hurt her ear. "I'm sorry. It was an accident."

Lacey yelled even louder. "YOU MUST NOT HAVE HEARD ME. YOU *RUINED* MY SWEATER!"

"I can hear you just fine," Marigold said quietly. "My hearing aid isn't broken. Your manners are."

"What did you just say?"

"I apologized already." Marigold's voice shook, but she didn't back down. "It was an accident. And you shouldn't make fun of my hearing."

Nory was impressed. Marigold was brave.

"I have a right to be upset," snarled Lacey. She gestured at her wet sweater. "I can't go through the school day like this."

"Don't Flares keep extra clothes in their lockers in case something gets burned?" said Nory. "Just go change."

Lacey twisted her face into an ugly shape. "How about if *you* just go *away*."

"It's only water."

"And you're only an upside-down wonko who doesn't know that wool isn't supposed to get wet." A new light came into Lacey's eyes. "Omigosh, you did this, didn't you?"

"Did what?"

Lacey swept her hand through the air. "The rocks. You fluxed the Pennies for Potions into rocks, didn't you?"

"No," Nory said. "That's not even possible."

"Then maybe Marigold shrank them. Did you, Marigold?"

"Then they would be *tiny pennies*," Marigold pointed out, laughing in disbelief. "Not rocks."

Lacey stepped forward and pushed her. "Don't laugh at me."

"Hey!" Marigold yelped.

Lacey went to push her again, and Marigold's

hand flew up. She grabbed Lacey's wrist, and the air shimmered around Marigold's fingers.

"Marigold! Stop!" cried Nory.

Marigold jerked her hand away, but it was too late. Lacey was already shrinking.

Smaller.

Smaller.

"I didn't mean to," Marigold cried. "I shrink things all the time by accident!"

Lacey's body shrank like a deflating balloon.

Her arms became tiny spindles.

Her head was the size of a cherry tomato.

Her teeny-tiny cardigan was still wet.

Finally, at three inches high, Lacey stopped shrinking.

Some of the kids gasped. Others laughed.

"You witch!" Lacey shrieked from down on the floor. Her voice was a squeak.

"She looks like a doll," a sixth grader said.

"Too small for a doll," another kid said.

Tiny Lacey stomped her tiny foot. "I am not a doll. Zinnia! Pick me up!"

Lacey's friend Zinnia moved in, looking horrified. She lifted Lacey gently between her thumb and forefinger and put her in the outside pocket of her backpack, which she left unzipped.

"Call my mother!" shouted Tiny Lacey. "Start a petition! Stop the upside-down magic! Call my father, too! Take me to the nurse! Take me to the principal! I want a dry sweater!"

Zinnia carried the backpack carefully toward Nurse Riley's office, followed by Rune. They walked on tiptoe to avoid the rocks.

Lacey's tiny voice could be heard for longer than Nory would have imagined. "Rune, get me a tissue! I want to dry off! Do you think we should call the newspaper? We'll need photographs, of course. Zinnia, I'm hungry. I want a grape. You're going to have to slice it into tiny pieces."

Marigold moaned. "I feel terrible."

Nory patted her arm. "Don't worry."

"You say that, but *you're* worried!" Marigold wailed. "I see it on your face!"

Nory tried to fix her features, but Marigold was right. Lacey Clench might be tiny, but she could still cause big trouble.

5

Nory watched as Principal Gonzalez reappeared with a team of teachers and janitors. They were armed with brooms, dustpans, and vacuum cleaners. They cleared the central hall of stones and began on the smaller hallways. Students started moving again. People shouldered their book bags and headed to class.

A girl's loud voice rang out. "Look! There's a huge rock in the middle of the hall!"

Oh, no, thought Nory. *Bax!*

She hurried over to where kids circled the rock. Elliott went with her.

"It's just our friend," Elliott said, pushing through. "We'll take care of him."

More kids swarmed around them.

"He's your friend?" someone said. "He's a rock!"

"He's an unusual Fluxer," said Nory. Her cheeks grew warm. "He's normally a boy."

"Can he turn other stuff into rocks?"

"No," said Nory. "His magic doesn't work like that."

"How do you know? Could he have turned the pennies into rocks? I bet that's how it happened!"

"That's not how it works," Nory insisted. "He fluxes his own body, like any other Fluxer."

But no one was listening to her. "I didn't believe they were dangerous, but now I'm getting nervous," someone said.

"What does this kid look like when he's human?" asked another. "We should know so we can stay away from him."

He said it in such a mean way that Nory felt like crying.

The crowd tightened around them: Nory, Elliott, and Rock-Bax. Nory wasn't sure what to do. She hoped she wouldn't accidentally flux. She hoped Elliott wouldn't ice anything.

"Nory, we need to get Bax out of here," Elliott said in a low voice.

But how?

"Excuse me!" The booming voice belonged to Principal Gonzalez. "I am ashamed of every single one of you," he said, striding over and breaking the group apart. "Do not gawk at a fluxed student. You all should know better. Everyone, get to class—now!"

Nory took one step before she felt Principal Gonzalez's hand on her shoulder. "Except you, Nory Horace. Please get the wheelbarrow and take Bax to the nurse's office."

Nory nodded and rolled it from her classroom.

This time, there was no back way.

This time everyone saw.

Nory could feel them all judging.

For Bax's sake, she held her head high.

In his office, Nurse Riley was as cheery as ever. He accepted Bax in the barrow, but left him in a corner for the time being.

Tiny Lacey was perched on the very edge of the cot. She glared at Nory.

"Yes, I'm still small," she said in a pinched voice. Her tiny arms were crossed across her tiny chest. Her tiny legs dangled over the vast distance between the cot and the floor. "The school will be hearing from my parents."

"Have you tried to unshrink her?" Nory asked the nurse.

Nurse Riley nodded. "She's looking at a trip to the hospital, I'm afraid. Her parents are sending an air taxi to transport her."

That was probably Aunt Margo. "Will the hospital doctors be able to fix her? Marigold couldn't unshrink her toothbrush. Or her grandpa's car," Nory said.

"Ah, but cars are cars and humans are humans. I bet they'll find a way. They have a lot more experience than Marigold. Lacey will probably have to be small for a couple more hours, but these things happen, don't they?"

"No!" cried Tiny Lacey. "These things *don't* happen! These wonkos are dangerous. They shouldn't be allowed at Dunwiddle!"

"Let's not get dramatic," Nurse Riley cautioned. "I treat a lot more burns caused by Flares than I do small people caused by Marigold."

Tiny Lacey snorted. "Those are not the same at all," she said, and pointed her puny finger at Nory. "You can tell Marigold that this is far from over."

Nory didn't know what to say.

So instead of talking, she fluxed into a dritten.

She jumped up on the infirmary cot and loomed her dritten body over Tiny Lacey. Dritten-Nory flapped her wings and bared her teeth. "Roar!"

Tiny Lacey screamed.

Nurse Riley picked up Dritten-Nory under her kitten armpits and held her at arm's length with one hand. With the other hand, he held her mouth closed so she couldn't breathe fire. He carried her out in the hall and set her down gently. He told her to flux back and that she owed Tiny Lacey an apology.

He was clearly annoyed.

Nory did as Nurse Riley asked, but she wasn't really sorry.

6

In the UDM classroom, everyone took a while to settle down. Ms. Starr, wearing wide-leg red pants and a turquoise sweater, declared that now was a good time for a trust exercise. The students all had to bring their chairs into a circle and hold hands. Ms. Starr gave Andres a back-pack full of bricks to wear, and strapped him to his chair with a bungee cord. Even so, he and the chair floated a couple of inches off the ground.

"Now we'll send a squeeze around the circle. I'll squeeze Pepper's hand, Pepper will squeeze

Willa's, and so on!" Ms. Starr said, smiling. "It's like a current of electricity uniting us."

Nory's hand felt sweaty. Bax still wasn't back from Nurse Riley's office. She squeezed Marigold's hand when Elliott squeezed hers.

She worried about the rocks in the hall.

She squeezed Marigold's hand when Elliott squeezed hers.

She worried about what Tiny Lacey would do for revenge.

She squeezed Marigold's hand when Elliott squeezed hers.

She turned into a puppy with squid legs.

Zamboozle! thought Squippy-Nory. *My tentacles are stuck to the floor. Am I still holding hands with—*

No. Elliott and Marigold had dropped Nory's squid legs. They were staring at her.

"What the zum-zum is that?" asked Marigold.

Excuse me? thought Nory. *Shouldn't Marigold*

be extra polite about wonky magic after what she did to Lacey this morning?

And also: *Ooh, that sneaker smells good. Maybe I should chew it. Yeah. Yeah.*

And then: *Who is that SCARY human wearing the sneaker?*

It was Pepper, of course. But Squippy-Nory couldn't understand that. She had lost control of her human mind. All she could think was: *Run! Hide!*

This was what Pepper's fiercing magic always did. It frightened animals and sent them yowling and howling for the hills.

Squippy-Nory scurried away from Pepper as fast as she could. *Where could she hide? Oh! Yes! Wide red pant leg! Just the right size for a frightened squippy.*

Squippy-Nory scuttled up Ms. Starr's leg and lodged herself in just below the knee, wrapping her tentacles around her teacher's calf. The calf smelled like vanilla body lotion and was wearing a stripy sock.

Ms. Starr patted Squippy-Nory's dog head through the fabric of her pants. "There, there, Nory," she said. "It's going to be okay. It's just Pepper. Can you remember your human mind? Pepper's your friend. She's not going to hurt you."

Squippy-Nory made doggy whimpering sounds.

There was a loud laugh.

Sebastian said, "Andres, your laugh looks like a huge hairy moth swooping around the room." Sebastian could *see* sound waves as well as hear them.

Someone else's laughter turned into a coughing fit.

"Elliott!" Marigold shrieked. "You spit on me!"

"There are icicles in your hair now," Andres said. "Elliott's spit turned to ice."

Marigold shrieked again, and Sebastian

moaned. "The shrieks look like steak knives! They're attacking me!"

"It's just ice," Willa said. "What's the big whoop?"

"It's Elliott's *spit*!" Marigold cried.

"Class! Children!" said Ms. Starr in a remarkably quiet voice. "I cannot walk with Nory's tentacles around my leg."

Everyone stopped laughing and shrieking. Nory was still a squippy, and she was still inside her teacher's pant leg.

"I do not want to shout when Sebastian is feeling sensitive to the sound waves," Ms. Starr went on. "We are all feeling sensitive this morning, don't you think? So let's be sensitive to our friends."

The room became silent. They *were* all feeling sensitive after the rocks in the hall and the shrinking of Lacey Clench.

"Pepper, I'm going to ask you and Sebastian

to go down the hall to the art supply room," continued Ms. Starr. "Please get me glitter, glue, sticks, and yarn. We're going to skip math this morning and do a therapeutic art project. Take a good long time about it, Pepper, okay? And we'll help Nory get back to her human self."

Squippy-Nory relaxed her tentacles a little bit and peeked out of the pant leg at the scary being. It was very small for such a CREATURE OF TERROR. It was looking down at the floor and sniffling a little bit as it walked to the door of the classroom.

A moment later, it was gone.

Phew. That was so much better.

Squippy-Nory didn't know what to do next. It was dark and warm in Ms. Starr's pant leg, and the squippy part of her thought staying right there was an excellent plan. The girl part of her didn't relish the idea of leaving the pant leg either. She'd have to face everyone. They'd laugh.

Marigold had said, "What the zum-zum."

But she knew she couldn't hide forever. She started down Ms. Starr's calf, moving backward inch by inch. Soon she felt fresh air on her tail and hindquarters.

"Elliott?" Ms. Starr said. "Can you come help remove Nory from my leg, please?"

With Pepper out of the room, Squippy-Nory wound her tentacles around Elliott's arm and gave him a doggy smile.

"You look totally cool," Elliott said kindly. "I never saw this one before."

And with Elliott being so nice and talking to her directly, as if he expected her human mind to understand, Nory flipped back to her girl self. She found herself hugging Elliott, and stepped back awkwardly.

Ms. Starr directed everyone to bring their chairs back to their desks and put on smocks. "That is enough hullabaloo for today, I think,"

Ms. Starr said. "Time to listen to Mozart and express ourselves with glitter."

"Do you want to hear an outrage?" Aunt Margo asked later that night.

It was evening, and Aunt Margo was home from work. She and Nory were eating pizza on the couch.

"Of course," Nory replied. She loved hearing Aunt Margo's outrages. Aunt Margo was a Flyer, and a very strong one. Unlike most Flyers, she could carry other people with her. That's how she'd ended up in her line of work. She ran a taxi service—but instead of driving a car, Aunt Margo *was* the taxi.

Often Margo's outrages involved people lying about the number of passengers when making reservations or people who insisted on having her carry their shopping bags on her ankles rather than holding them themselves. But this time,

Nory suspected the outrage was something a little closer to her own day.

"The pickup was at your school, actually." Aunt Margo talked with her mouth full. That was something Father didn't allow back home. He didn't allow eating in front of the TV or putting your feet on the coffee table, either.

Nory had lived with Aunt Margo for a month now. She missed Hawthorn and Dalia, her brother and sister. She missed Father, too, she supposed. But she didn't miss Father's endless list of rules.

"This horrid man called me at the last minute. Mr. Clench. And he didn't want to pay full fare. He asked me to fly his daughter from school to the hospital—in the rain, I might add—and he wanted to pay just a quarter of the usual price."

Nory's heart thumped. She knew it. Clench! The horrid man was Lacey's father!

"He was in a tizzy because his daughter was

three inches high. She'd had some sort of magical accident. Maybe I'm being too hard on him," Aunt Margo said. "But it wasn't a medical *emergency*, and he couldn't seem to grasp that I charge for travel time, with no discount for tiny passengers. 'Thirty minutes is thirty minutes,' I told him."

"Did Lacey get fixed?" Nory asked. "Is she back to her normal size?"

"I don't know. I left after dropping her off," Margo said. "But she was healthy as can be, aside from being so small. Oh! And she blamed your friend Marigold, but I couldn't get a straight story out of her. She was quite a little ball of hostility, that one." Margo rearranged her feet on the coffee table, crossing her ankles. "Now, what do *you* know about the whole business?"

Nory stuffed a big bite of pizza in her mouth to buy herself time. She wasn't sure what she wanted to say. When she'd been with Father, the family hadn't talked much about upside-down magic. In fact, they tried not to mention anything uncomfortable, ever.

Aunt Margo was more open. She was Nory's mother's sister. (Nory's mother had died a long time ago.) Even though Aunt Margo thought about things very differently than Father did, Nory still wasn't sure she wanted to share how badly things had gone today.

"I don't get along with Lacey Clench," she finally said. "But guess what? I'm going to join beginner kittenball. There's a club at school."

"Kittenball?" Aunt Margo said. "I *love* kittenball."

"You do?"

"Your mother was a great swatter. I used to go to all her games. She was on an all-state champion team in high school. It helped get her into that fancy college, and there she got licensed for a tiger. That was a serious tiger, let me tell you.

I do not like large carnivores in the house with me, even if they are my blood relatives. We used to share a bedroom when she was back from school. I'd walk in and there'd be a tiger sitting in front of the vanity, examining its own pretty fur."

Wow. Nory knew her mom had been a Fluxer, but she had never known about the tiger, or the kittenball.

"I think she could have played professionally, if she hadn't met your dad and gotten interested in becoming a doctor. Anyway, she was a great player. You should have seen her pounce when the yarnball came her way."

"The coach is really nice," said Nory. "He invited me to sign up. There's only one problem."

"What's that?"

"I don't know the rules."

Aunt Margo grinned. "There's a tigerball

game on tonight. Start of the season, Stripeys versus Pouncers. Shall we watch? And have popcorn? I'll explain the rules to you. We can invite Figs over—he loves a good tigerball game."

And so they did. Aunt Margo's boyfriend, Figs, brought some cinnamon rolls he'd baked.

"See the tower in the middle of the court?" Aunt Margo asked.

Nory nodded.

"On top of the tower is a basket. Each team has nine yarnballs—nine chances to score."

"Got it," Nory said. She took a big bite of cinnamon roll.

"The Pouncers are up!" Figs hollered. Like Nory, Figs was a Fluxer. His preferred animal was a Saint Bernard. Right now he was an olive-skinned human wearing jeans and a blue Pouncers jersey.

"Okay," Aunt Margo said. "It's the Pouncers'

yarnball. They're the ones wearing blue collars. They have to start at the edge of the court, pass the yarnball, climb it up the tower, and drop it in the net. But, see, at the same time, the Stripeys— the tigers in white collars—are trying to stop them from scoring by unspooling their yarn."

On the screen, the Stripeys were whacking the yarnball out of the Pouncers' paws. Blue yarn was now strung across the court.

"As soon as there's no more yarn left, it's the other team's ball," she added. "They get a fresh yarnball in their team color."

"The Pouncers are going for it!" Figs cried. "They're climbing up the tower! They're going to—"

"Score!" they all cheered.

The three of them cheered the Pouncers to victory.

There were ladybugs in Bax's dad's house. Not

one ladybug, but eight—no, nine ladybugs. They weren't flying or sitting among the plants. It seemed like they were watching television. They were all together on the arm of the couch, near Bax's dad's favorite spot.

"Are you doing something Fuzzy with these, or should I put them outside?" Bax asked. His dad was a Fuzzy, but he was allergic to fur, so they didn't have any pets.

"Whatever you want," his dad said.

"Couldn't you just ask them to fly outside?"

His dad shook his head. "I'm too tired. Why don't you scoop them into a cup?"

Bax put the ladybugs outside in the backyard. Then he practiced piano and folded laundry on the living room floor while Dad fixed cheese toast and pickles for dinner. Bax's parents had divorced a year ago. Not long after, Bax had turned ten and fluxed into a rock.

Bax had been hoping to be a Flicker, like his

mom, or a Flyer, like a couple of his friends from ordinary school. Whatever magic came, he'd known it would show up soon—he just hadn't been expecting to miss it when it happened.

One minute he'd been sitting outside, licking a chocolate ice-cream cone. The next thing he knew, he was awake at the hospital, with the bitter taste of Burtlebox in his mouth.

Bax's mom had met them at the hospital. It was awkward and sad, since his parents didn't live together anymore. Bax had gone back to his mom's house with several bottles of Burtlebox and a long list of safety precautions.

Not long after, his dad had heard about the Upside-Down Magic program starting at Dunwiddle. He had rented a new house near the school. It was a nice house, but it still felt kind of empty.

Bax thought his dad felt a little empty, too. But he didn't know how to talk about that. They had eaten cheese toast for dinner for a week now. That made Bax think something was wrong. Then his dad sat down at the table and said, "I have to tell you something"—and Bax knew it for sure.

"Okay." Bax felt scared. "What?"

"I lost my job."

His dad worked in the office of the local art museum, with a bunch of computers. Bax didn't really understand what he did.

"Oh." Bax's heart sank. "I wondered why you were home early."

"I got let go last week."

"I wondered why you got home early every day last week, too."

"I was hoping to find a new job before I had to tell you. But that hasn't happened yet."

"Why'd they let you go?"

"They had a lot of layoffs. I didn't do any-thing wrong. They just don't need me anymore."

"Can you get another job?"

"Of course. I hope."

"Will we run out of money?"

"I have savings. Don't worry."

"Can't you take allergy pills?" Bax asked. "Then you could use your Fuzzy skills. Or maybe you could get a job at an aquarium?"

A few years ago, they had gone together to the Ocean Blue Aquarium, and it was amazing for Bax to watch his dad communicate with the schools of leaping rainbow and parrot fish. They had tried to dance behind him as he bounced through the room.

"I'm out of practice with magic," Dad said. "I'll have to find a job that requires my smarts instead."

"Let's watch the tigerball game," Bax suggested. He made his voice eager, to cheer up his dad. "Okay?"

"Stripeys for the win," Dad said, forcing a

smile. "The Pouncers don't have a chance."

They brought their cheese toast to the couch and watched the game. By the end, there were four more red ladybugs sitting next to Dad.

The Stripeys lost.

Bax's mom picked him up in the morning and drove him to Cider Cup by the Sea, where she worked as a police detective. Her house was where the whole family had lived until the divorce. These days, Bax spent Saturday nights and Tuesday nights with his mom. The rest of the time he stayed with his dad, who lived closer to school.

It was hard. The shirt he wanted to wear was always at the wrong parent's house.

Saturday night, he and his mom watched a movie. Bax picked a funny one with lots of car chases. His mom was a Flicker and was good with light, so the movie she ordered online was projected huge on the white wall of her living room.

On Sunday, Bax had a piano lesson and then turned into a rock again while she drove him home. He woke up in bed at his dad's house, with the taste of Burtlebox coating his tongue.

The next morning, Bax's dad was quiet. He scrambled eggs for them both, but he didn't listen to the radio news or ask about the upcoming week. Bax got his backpack ready and put on his jacket. "Bye," he said, hovering at his dad's side. He wanted to hug him, or talk to him, but he didn't know how to start.

"Bye," said his dad glumly.

Bax trudged out the front door. On the stoop sat a chipmunk, looking mopey. It sniffed at the front door, then looked at Bax with big chipmunk eyes.

"You can't go in there," said Bax. "The house is not for chipmunks."

The chipmunk slumped.

"Go play," said Bax.

The chipmunk lay down on its tummy on the welcome mat.

"You can't go in," said Bax. "Sheesh."

The chipmunk heaved a sigh. It didn't move from its place on the mat.

"Fine," Bax said, heading down the sidewalk. "Do whatever you want."

He looked back after several yards. The chipmunk was still there.

7

At school that day, Nory, Pepper, and Marigold were behind Lacey Clench on the salad bar line. Lacey was back to normal size.

She took a serving of carrots and spun around.

So did Rune, and so did Zinnia.

Nory, Pepper, and Marigold backed up.

"Did you know I was at the hospital for *five hours* on Friday night?" Lacey said, putting her hands on her hips. "*And* I had to get ten shots, because that's how old I am. They had to regrow me, which totally hurt, and I had to drink eighteen cups of coconut water over the course of the five hours, to flush out my system."

"I *am* really sorry," said Marigold. "I know you think I did it on purpose, but I didn't. I swear."

"Says you," Lacey snapped.

"Lacey's started a petition," Rune said. "She already has three signatures."

"A *petition?*" Pepper said.

"I don't sit around complaining," said Lacey. "I like to get things done."

Pepper spread her hands. "But a petition for what?"

"To get the UDM program removed from Dunwiddle," said Lacey. "And the UDM students removed as well. I think we'll get a lot of support." Lacey smiled. "You're a danger to the rest of us."

"You're way more dangerous than we are," Nory snapped. "You're the one who did unauthorized flaring and burned Andres's leash. He could have died."

Lacey sneered. "Last year, when the Flicker students wanted to get an invisible diving coach and start a team using the high school pool, they wrote a proposal and got fifty signatures. And you know what?"

"What?"

"This year there's an invisible diving team, that's what. Principal Gonzalez had to make one. Because the Flickers got the signatures. And when I reach fifty, I'm giving the petition to him, and your wonko program will be going, going, gone." Lacey stamped her back-to-normal-size foot. "Forever."

That afternoon, Nory went to after-school kittenball club. She was excited and curious. She tried not to think about Lacey Clench's petition.

Three other beginner Fluxers showed up. Nory didn't know them. She didn't know any of the Fluxers in her grade, besides Bax.

Akari, Finn, and Paige didn't know Nory, either, it seemed. At least, there was no finger-pointing or whispering.

Coach started by having them all drink a glass of pomegranate juice and eat a bit of dried seaweed. "Good for muscle tone," he said.

Then he asked them to introduce themselves and flux briefly into the kitten shapes they'd be practicing with today. "The size of your kitten doesn't matter," he said, "but nimble paws and strong tails make for a good player."

The Fluxers all had reliable kitten shapes. Nory was impressed. Akari played as a tabby. Paige did a ginger cat with a lovely orange tail. Finn was black with white paws. Nory fluxed into her basic black kitten and kept the form nicely.

"I can't always hold it past fifteen minutes," she told them when she popped back. "But Coach said I should try kittenball anyhow."

"I pop back to human sometimes, too," said Paige. She was pale and tall, with cute freckles. She wore her long brown hair in a fancy Dutch braid. "Cats aren't easy for me. Honestly, I do better with things in the rodent family. But I'm working on it. Practice makes perfect, right?" She smiled hopefully.

Paige assumes I'm a typical Fluxer, Nory thought. *She must think I'm a sixth grader. She doesn't seem to know my magic is upside down.* It felt good to have her not know. But it also felt a bit like a lie.

Coach went off to get the yarnballs from the shed, and Finn threw himself onto the grass in human form. "Where did they put all those rocks after they cleaned up?" he wondered. "Does anyone know?"

"It wasn't worth trying to turn them back, I heard, so they carted them to the ordinary school and used them for gravel in the garden," Paige said.

"Those UDM kids better stop messing around," said Akari. "They're getting people scared."

Nory tensed.

"I'd like to know which one of them did it," Finn said thoughtfully. "But even more, I'd like to know how."

"They might have all done it together," Akari said.

"The real problem is that one of them shrank that Flare girl to three inches high."

"Was she okay?" asked Akari.

"She was fine," said Nory. "She's back to normal size."

"Yeah," said Finn. "But did you hear that the girl who got shrunk is going around with a *petition* now? She wants the upside-down program moved out of Dunwiddle."

"Did you sign it?" Akari asked.

"Not yet, but I'm thinking about it," said Finn.

"Because of the shrinking and the rocks. Those kids might be dangerous."

"And remember when there was that weird animal in the cafeteria? It was, like, part skunk and part *elephant*. Nothing like that ever happened in ordinary school," said Akari.

Nory felt ill. And embarrassed. And a little angry.

Paige turned. "Nory, you should see your face. What's wrong?"

"Me? Nothing."

"Seriously," Paige pressed. "What are you thinking?"

Nory gathered her courage. "I hear what you're saying. Because the rocks were weird, and when Lacey shrank, that was scary. But—"

"Kittenballers! Hup!" Coach was striding across the field with a bag of yarnballs. It was time to practice. Nory stopped talking.

Coach explained the techniques of offense and defense. A kitten should use its tail to whack the yarnball to a teammate, but the quickest way to unspool the other team's yarn was to pin the yarn with one front paw and roll the ball away with the other.

Akari and Finn fluxed into their kittens. Coach put a purple yarnball in between them and ordered them to whack it back and forth. He tossed an orange ball for Paige and Nory to work with. They, too, fluxed into their kitten shapes.

"Remember," Coach said. "When you're passing your own team's ball, you don't want to unwind it."

Paige leapt at the yarnball and whacked it toward Nory with her tail.

Nory batted it back with a satisfying smack. Practice was fun! She could do this!

The ball returned to her a few seconds later, and this time she whacked it with her tail. *Boom!*

Some of the orange yarn had unspooled around her feet. She lifted her paws high, trying to escape the tangle, but before she could, Paige slammed what was left of the yarnball her way.

Nory swatted at it, but her front legs were tied up in yarn.

As was her tail.

Oh, and one of her hind feet.

She was trapped! Ahh!

Panic!

Pop! Pop! Pop!

Before she could stop it, her body started to flux. Nory was shrinking—smaller than she'd ever shrunk before. And as she shrank, she grew wings. Not the dragon wings she was used to, and not the bluebird wings she'd done now and then. These were filmy, delicate wings—followed by a long, tubular nose on her kitten face.

Her legs grew thin and spindly, coming out of her furry kitten torso.

Was she a mosquito?

Yes! She was!

Well, part mosquito, part kitten.

Mitten?

She was so tiny she flew right out of the yarn.

Paige snapped back to human form in shock. "Nory! What's happening?"

Mmm, that girl smells delicious, Mitten-Nory thought. *Mmm. After-school snack.*

No! Girl-Nory told herself sternly. *Your new kittenball friend is a not a snack. No, no, no!*

"Coach!" Paige yelled. She tugged at the sleeves of her shirt, trying to cover her skin. "Come quick! Something's wrong with Nory! I think she fluxed into an insect!"

Coach hurried over.

Akari and Finn switched back to human form. *Mmm.* Now they smelled delicious, too.

"Nory!" Coach said. "Can you hear me? Come here! Now!"

Girl-Nory heard the command. She flew over to Coach.

He *didn't* smell good. Too much herbal tea in his bloodstream, probably. Also kind of sweaty.

Coach held out his hand. Nory landed on it. He peered at her. He stroked his chin. "Look at you!" he said. "Fascinating. Three-quarters mosquito and only one-quarter kitten. Have you ever done an insect before? I had a girlfriend in college who could do mosquito and centipede. Separately, of course."

Akari came closer, and Mitten-Nory stopped paying attention to Coach. Oh, what a plump and juicy arm that Akari had! Mitten-Nory flew into the air to buzz closer. Blooooooooooood!

Akari backed away.

Blooooooood!

"Nory!" Coach yelled. "Turn back now. You're losing your human mind!"

Pop! Nory's shame made her switch back.

Oh, drat.

So embarrassing.

Being a mitten was really, really wonky.

Nory patted her body to make sure she was all in proper girl shape.

"That was—I never saw anything like it," Paige said. "You were a kitten. And then . . ." She took a step back. "Are you one of those upside-down kids?"

Nory looked at her. "Well, yes. But you're wrong about us. We're not dangerous."

"Her mosquito wanted to bite me!" Akari cried.

Coach shrugged. "Relax, Akari. Nory was less than an inch long. The worst she could have done was make you itch."

"I should have told you all earlier," said Nory, her cheeks on fire. "Coach knows. But I should have spoken up. I'm sorry."

Paige's expression softened. "You know what?

We were the rude ones. We kept going on about the UDM kids, and we didn't even think you might be one of them. I'm sorry."

Nory felt a huge wave of relief. "That's okay," she said. "I'm sorry I turned into a mitten during practice."

Paige nodded, as if she'd made up her mind about something. "Look, I'm glad to have another girl at kittenball. And you seem cool. Just don't bite me, okay?"

"Okay."

Paige tossed a yarnball into the air and caught it neatly. "In that case, want to get back to tail-whacking?"

Nory grinned, then fluxed into a black kitten. "Meow."

8

Bax hated Dunwiddle School's tuna noodle casserole. He stood in line, but only took potato chips, canned peaches, and then some raw broccoli from the salad bar. He carried his tray over to sit with the other UDM kids at one big table. Nory had called a meeting.

Nory looked around, as if making sure all eight of them were there. Andres had a bag lunch and floated above. The other seven were all seated. "What are we going to do about Lacey's petition?" she asked.

"It's my fault for shrinking her," said Marigold.

She poked her casserole with her fork instead of eating it.

Bax felt bad for Marigold. He knew what it was like to have out-of-control magic.

"Do you think you can make it up to Lacey somehow?" Willa wondered. "Get her to forget about the petition?"

"I doubt it," Elliott said. And he would know—he and Lacey had been friends in ordinary school, until she and the other Sparkies shunned him because of his freezing magic.

"I talked to Principal Gonzalez," said Marigold. "I told him I'd take whatever consequence I deserved."

"What did he say?" Pepper asked.

"He said not to worry about it and that he would talk to Lacey's family. He said he knew it was an accident."

"Hey, people, I'm having a birthday party!" called Andres from the ceiling. "It's this Saturday at two, and all of you are invited!"

Andres hardly ever heard much of what went on during cafeteria conversations. He was eating a sandwich, dropping crumbs on people and occasionally calling down random remarks.

Nory looked up. "Sounds fun, Andres! I'll come!"

"Me too," Bax said. He'd be at his mom's, but Bax knew she'd drive him to Andres's.

The other kids said they'd be at the party as well. Nory brought the conversation back to Lacey.

"The shrinking isn't the big problem," she said. "The real issue is the rocks, because they affected so many people. The kids from kitten-ball think we did it."

"What do you mean, 'we'?" Sebastian said. "Like, all of us?" He glanced from face to face. "Listen. *Was* it any of you guys? It wasn't me, I swear."

"Or me," said Marigold.

"Or me," said Willa.

"Or me," said Elliott.

The other kids proclaimed their innocence one by one, until Bax was the only person left.

"It wasn't me, either!" he said. But his friends were looking at him funny. His stomach flipped over. "What? It wasn't!"

"Bax, you're the one with rock magic. Have you *ever* turned anything else to stone?" Elliott asked carefully. "Anything other than your own body?"

"Never!" Bax said. His voice cracked.

Elliott said, "Right. Okay. Just checking."

"Never," Bax insisted. A lump formed in his throat, and he dug his fingernails into his palms. He *hadn't* turned other things to stone. His magic didn't work that way.

"What if it was a prank?" Willa asked. "Principal Gonzalez said something about the eighth graders, how they prank the school every year. They *said* they didn't do the stones, but would they admit it if they did?"

"When my sister was in eighth grade," Sebastian commented, "the eighth-grade Flickers made all the toilets disappear. I mean, they were still there, but nobody could see them. Then people stopped flushing after they used them, because that was the only way they could see where the toilets were. Everything got really disgusting."

Andres called down from the ceiling. "The rocks weren't an eighth-grade prank. My sister, Carmen, is in eighth now and she swears it wasn't."

"Is she trustworthy?" Elliott called up.

Andres huffed. "She's in the honor society!"

"So we're right back where we started," Nory said. "It wasn't us, but it looks like us, because no one else has wonky magic."

"Don't say *wonky*," Willa said automatically. "Say *unusual*."

Bax felt itchy.

It seemed like Elliott secretly thought it was him. It seemed like everyone secretly thought it was him.

But it wasn't.

At tutoring, Coach wanted to talk to Nory. And only Nory.

Bax was not surprised.

"The mitten was exciting, and I'm happy to know you can do it, but let's face it," said Coach, "you could get squashed. And most people don't master insect forms until college, if they do them at all. There are a lot of complications. So let's see that dritten of yours again."

Nory bit her lip. "I think I should work on just plain kitten some more. So I can learn to stop other animals from popping out."

"No, no. Do dritten," Coach said.

"I don't want to fire-breathe on you. If you want something upside-down, I guess I could do the squippy again."

"Dritten!" barked Coach.

"He wants you to practice it for kittenball," Bax muttered. "He wants a winning team."

Nory shrugged. Then, with a popping noise and a *whoomp*, she fluxed. Her black kitten body was glossy, and her whiskers were perky. It wasn't long, though, before the wings sprouted from her back and filled the room with a rushing sound as they flapped and lifted her up. Her claws popped out. Her teeth looked dangerous.

Bax sucked in his breath. Dritten-Nory wasn't that big, but she was scary.

"Go, Nory!" Coach cheered.

Dritten-Nory did not seem to have control of her human mind. She knocked over a case of kittenball trophies with the tip of her powerful wing.

She flared her kitten nostrils, opened her mouth full of dragon teeth, and breathed fire at Coach's shoes.

"Wow!" Coach said. He hopped from foot to foot, and the smell of burnt leather filled the room. "You see that, Bax? Fire!"

Bax walked glumly over to the fire extinguisher and sprayed the carpet.

At the sound of the extinguisher, Dritten-Nory scrambled her kitten paws in the air as if trying to swim. Then with a thump, she fell hard to the floor.

She was in girl form again.

"Fantastic!" Coach said.

"I wasn't in control," Nory cried. "I almost hurt you."

"The kitten body was fully recognizable as kitten," said Coach. "No one could argue. I'll have to double-check the regulations, but the Twinkle Tidbits have a six-toed kitten on their team, so I don't see that wings are any different."

"I set your shoe on fire!" yelled Nory. "It is not safe to be a dritten!"

"Oh, we'll get it sorted with practice," said Coach. "Don't be a worrywart. You're going to be a kittenball legend, Nory Horace. Tigerball legend, I should say. Really, you could go pro with that thing."

"What about Bax?" Nory said.

"What about who?"

Nory pointed.

"Oh! Him! *Bax*, yes!" Coach said.

Bax smiled grimly. *Yep, me, the other person in the room. I just put out a fire on your foot and you still didn't know I was here.*

"What about him?" Coach said.

"What do you want him to do?" said Nory.

Coach faced Bax. "Flux, please."

"Not today," Bax mumbled.

"See?" Coach said to Nory. "I can give him

carrot juice and flaxseed, certainly. But how can I help him if he won't show me what he can do?"

"But it's tutoring for *both* of us," Nory said.

"Nory—" Bax said.

"No, Bax, for real," Nory snapped. "You want to get your magic together. I know you do, because I know how much *I* want to get mine together."

Bax got the lump in his throat again.

"Bax. Come on. Show him," coaxed Nory. "So he can help."

Nory and Coach waited. They kept their eyes glued to him.

"Can you flux for me, son?" Coach said. It was almost gentle.

Bax did want Coach's help. He felt ashamed of wanting Coach's help, but what else was new? He felt ashamed about turning into a rock, too. A deep heaviness filled Bax's body. His bones felt stiff.

Then he fluxed.

The next thing Bax knew, he was in the nurse's office.

Of course. As usual.

Coach was there with Nurse Riley. Nory stood there, too. "Coach said I should stay," she explained, when Bax gave her a look. "He said we were a team, the three of us, and I should stick around."

Coach put his hands on his legs and bent closer to Bax. He peered into Bax's eyes. "Do you particularly like rocks?" he asked.

Bax shook his head.

"What about rock candy? Do you like rock candy?"

Bax looked at him funny. Nurse Riley did, too.

"What?" Coach said. "Rock candy has no nutritional value. None! If a child was to eat a lot of rock candy, who's to say what might happen?"

"Does Nory eat a lot of kittens?" Bax asked. He hesitated, then went for it. "Do *you?*"

Nory burst out laughing.

"Fine, fine," Coach said gruffly. "But nutrition could be a factor here."

"I hadn't considered that," said Nurse Riley. "Maybe he can keep a food diary."

Coach sat on a stool, his muscly bulk awkward on the small seat. "Bax. Let me get everything clear. No one knows why you flux the way you do. Is that what I'm to understand?"

Bax nodded.

"It's happening more and more," Nurse Riley added. He held up the Burtlebox and pursed his lips. "The doctor had this potion formulated just for Bax, and it does work. His parents give it to him at home as well. He takes it more often than I'd like, though. With these individual potions, you don't always know how a person's body will react with long-term use."

"I'm fine," said Bax. "It doesn't bother me. It just tastes bad."

Coach clapped his hand on Bax's shoulder. It felt heavy and warm. "Listen here, son. I've not given you the attention you deserve, but we're going to figure this out. Ms. Starr, Nurse Riley, and I are on your team! Teamwork is the answer in kittenball, and it's the answer here as well."

Bax wanted to believe him. He met Coach's gaze.

"What does it feel like when you flux, son?" Coach asked.

"Before I flux, I feel heavy. Then I feel nothing. And then it hurts, after."

"What do you mean, nothing?"

"I don't feel *anything*," Bax said. "I can't hear, can't move, can't smell. It's like I'm not even there. Not the *me* part of me."

"Hmm," Coach said. "You flux a lot by accident, but you can also choose to flux on purpose. Yes? Yes. That's an excellent starting point. Are you always a rock?"

"Every time but once," Bax said. He paused. "I fluxed into a leash—"

"A leash!"

"On purpose, too. Because Andres needed me."

"It was amazing," Nory said.

Bax blushed. "But I've never done that again."

"How did you do it that one time?" Nurse Riley asked.

"I don't know. I mean, I wanted to—and I just did. And then I got stuck, like always."

Nurse Riley nodded.

"Here's what we're going to do," Coach said. "First, I want you to write down what you eat and when you flux. Like a schedule, see? We can see if you have any allergies that are making it hard for you. After we check for allergies, I'm going to have you start eating seaweed and sardines and other high-nutrient foods. At the same time, I'll teach you some tricks to help you hold on to your human mind as you flux. I have some ideas that might help. After that, you can work on doing that leash again, but this time, you'll hold on to your human mind when you do it. Sound good?"

Bax nodded.

"I'm going to work with Ms. Starr on this," Coach said. "It'll get better, son."

"Will it?" Bax said. He heard the hope in his voice, and his face grew warm.

Coach squeezed Bax's shoulder. "It will."

Coach left. Nurse Riley told Bax he wanted to take his temperature, but then another student came in, a Fuzzy who had gotten a very small toad stuck up her nose. Nurse Riley had to take her into the back room to extract it.

He left Nory and Bax alone.

"So I guess we should keep food diaries," Nory said, kicking her feet as she sat on the cot. "To see if we have allergies or need more protein to be good Fluxers, or whatever."

"You don't have to," Bax said. "Coach said just me."

"It's only fair that we both do it," Nory said. "Though maybe I'll write down that I'm eating a regular diet of kittens, just to mess with Coach."

Bax smiled. "I'll write about eating gravel."

"Ew."

"What about puppies? And goats? And squid? Are you gonna tell him you eat those, too?"

"Of course," Nory said. "Also dragons. But only, like, once a week."

"Careful with dragons," Bax warned. "I hear they're really spicy."

They both started laughing.

Nurse Riley returned to the room. "What's so

funny in here?" he asked. He held a tiny toad in a pair of tweezers. He put it gently into a small plastic terrarium with air holes.

"Nory, don't eat that toad, please," said Bax. "It's supposed to go back to the Fuzzy lab."

"I wouldn't eat *that* one," said Nory, giggling. "That one's been in someone's nose! Don't be gross."

Nurse Riley shook his head as he took Bax's temperature on his forehead. "Your temperature's healthy," he said. "Though your brain is maybe deranged."

9

Bax's mom drove him to Andres's house on Saturday afternoon. Everyone from the UDM class was there when he arrived.

It was a warm and welcoming house, and Bax was interested to see how the Padillo family had adapted things to his friend's floating situation. There were enormous bags of bricks in every room, heavy enough to keep Andres down when needed. Andres's bed was nailed to the ceiling. His sheets and comforter were strapped into place with a big elastic band. A set of bongos and some other drums were attached to the ceiling in one corner.

Mr. and Mrs. Padillo were very friendly, and Andres's sister, Carmen, had put together party games in the basement rec room. Stomp the balloon! (Sebastian had to wear his blindfold—the sound waves were intense.) Freeze tag! (When Elliott was It, he accidentally froze Willa's hair for real.)

Back upstairs, everyone had pineapple upside-down cake (of course). Nory and Bax wrote it in their food diaries. Also, cheese-flavored potato chips, barbecue potato chips, ranch-flavored potato chips, regular potato chips, and corn chips.

Then Andres opened presents on the ceiling. He carefully handed the gifts to his parents to put on the kitchen table, but wrapping paper remnants drifted slowly down and landed on the guests.

"Andres, do you live near Lacey Clench?"

asked Pepper, removing green ribbon from her hair.

"No, but Rune lives down at the end of my block."

"Ah, that must be it," Pepper said. "I saw the Sparkies in a tree house on my way here."

"Rune has a tree house, all right," said Elliott. "I used to go there all the time, back when we were friends." A shadow crossed his face. "Back when I *thought* we were friends."

"I used to see you there sometimes, remember?" said Andres. "In ordinary school, before my magic came in, Rune and I hung out all the time, because of how close our houses are."

"I wonder if they're plotting against us," said Nory.

Bax lowered his voice. "We could spy on them," he ventured. "If we wanted to find out what they're plotting."

"You are an evil genius, Bax Kapoor," Nory said.

Bax flushed with pride.

"The most important thing is stealth," said Bax, a couple of minutes later. The UDM kids were a few houses down from Rune's, huddled together and buzzing with nerves. "Nory, you flux into a kitten," he instructed. Bax's mom was a detective, after all. She had told him about stakeouts. "No bitten, no mitten, no koat, no dritten, no funny business," he went on. "Can you do it and stay kitten-shaped?"

Nory nodded. "No bitten, no mitten, no koat, no dritten."

"Good," said Bax. "You do that and then climb up the tree and *act like an actual kitten*. Stay hidden! Andres, you need camouflage. We're going to decorate you with leaves."

"Someone still needs to hold my leash," said Andres.

"I will," said Willa.

Bax found some leaves and vines to camouflage Andres and Willa. "Now, does anyone want to be shrunk by Marigold? That would be a great detective move."

"I am *not* doing that to anyone again," said Marigold. "I refuse."

"Okay. It was just an idea," said Bax. "It could be a really useful talent for police work, you know."

Marigold smiled.

"Everyone ready?" said Bax. "Nory, flux! Andres, pull that one twig a little farther over your shirt—perfect. Willa, sneak into the bushes and let Andres float up near the tree house. The rest of us will be just around the corner in case you need backup. Go, go, go!"

Nory liked the idea of being a detective on a stakeout. Lots of detectives were Fluxers. She fluxed into an ordinary kitten and climbed as close as she could to Rune's tree house.

Lacey was holding court. "I was practically trampled four times that day," she said. "And everyone looked like ugly giants. They were so big."

"Except really *you* were small," said Zinnia. "And also, we've heard all this before."

"Zinnia?" Lacey said sharply. "Watch it."

Zinnia bowed her head. She sat beside Lacey. On Lacey's other side sat Rune and two other kids from the fifth-grade Flare class.

They've added to their ranks, Girl-Nory thought. *Not good.*

The talk continued, and this larger group of Sparkies had plenty of negative things to say about all the UDM kids. They said Marigold should be kept home from school because of how dangerous she was. They made fun of Sebastian and how he ducked to avoid the sound waves in gym class. They called Pepper "cruel to animals" and mocked Elliott.

"He tried to roast a marshmallow once, and it just froze into a Popsicle!" Rune laughed. Nory hoped Elliott couldn't hear him.

"That skunk-elephant girl is disgusting," said one of the new recruits. "She's the one who's really wonko."

"That's Nory Horace," said Zinnia.

"Can she do other wonko shapes? Someone in the lunchroom said something about a mosquito kitten."

"Gross!"

At that moment, Girl-Nory wanted to try for the driger—dragon-tiger—and show these kids what scary *really* meant.

But then she'd blow her cover.

And she might burn them.

Or eat them.

She probably couldn't even do a driger. She didn't have tiger yet.

So she kept quiet, even though she liked what

they said next even less.

"Bax," Lacey was saying, "is as dumb as a box of rocks."

"Instead of playing rock, paper, scissors," Rune went on, "he probably plays rock, rock, rock—and still loses. And then there's Willa. She rains anytime anyone says boo to her. She's the biggest crybaby in the world." He laughed.

Kitten-Nory couldn't say anything, but she looked down at Willa in the bushes and saw tears running down her face.

Andres was tangled in the tree branches. Nory couldn't see his expression.

"Enough complaining. Let's get something *done*," Lacey said. "We've all signed the petition, but we need to get more people. Too many people are saying no to me. That's why we have to think about what the worst things those UDM guys could do. Then we need to *make* them *do* those things."

"How?" asked Zinnia.

"By making them mad or teasing them or whatever—and we need to make sure everyone sees. If they mess up in a really big way, people will agree they don't belong at Dunwiddle."

"Willa's an easy target," one of the new Sparkies said. "The indoor rain does a lot of damage."

"That Pepper girl can do more than she lets on, I'm sure," Rune said. "I bet she can force animals to do things for her, out of fear. We could, I don't know, go to the Fuzzy lab, release all the animals, and then get Pepper to scare them so they wreck stuff."

"What about Elliott?" Rune said. "He turns stuff to ice. How could we use that? What would be the worst thing we could get him to freeze? How big can he go? Let's make him do something terrible!"

There was a rustling in the tree. A frantic shaking of branches. "What kind of person are you?" Andres shouted at Rune. "Elliott brought peanut butter cookies up to this very tree house! I was there! You ate them!"

"Andres?" Rune said. Nory saw him look from side to side.

"Yes! Remember me?" He'd totally lost his temper, and the branches were going crazy.

They had to get him out of the tree. Nory leapt down to the sidewalk and fluxed back into a girl. She grabbed Willa's hand. "Come on!"

"Hey!" Rune called, looking down from the floor of the tree house. "They were spying on us!"

Nory and Willa pulled on Andres's leash, but Andres was caught in the branches.

They yanked.

Andres yelped.

They yanked again.

Then five Sparkie faces appeared over the walls of the tree house. All five faces were angry.

Nory and Willa yanked again, even harder this time. Finally, Andres came loose from the branches with a crackling of wood. Leaves fell everywhere.

"Run!" he screamed.

10

Get them!" the Sparkies cried. They swarmed down from the tree house.

Nory and Willa fled from the yard. Andres bobbed behind, trailing leaves and bits of vine. They got to the street where the rest of the UDM kids were.

"Go, go, go!" Nory cried.

They charged up the block. Andres kicked wildly through the air.

Nory looked over her shoulder. Lacey was a grim bulldozer, running in front of the Sparkies pack.

Nory felt heat on her neck. The sound of

pounding feet rose and roared behind her. Lacey grabbed the collar of her shirt and jerked.

"You are so going down, Nory Horace," Lacey panted.

Nory tugged free and ran, but a flaming tennis ball whizzed past her ear. Then another. Then another.

Unsupervised flaring! Horrible!

Marigold reached out a hand and tapped one of the flaming balls as it zipped by. It shrank to almost nothing! She did the same to the next one.

Unsupervised shrinking! Awesome!

Elliott iced a tennis ball and kept running. But more tennis balls came, orange streaks of flame behind them.

One scorched Nory's ear. Another burned Sebastian's elbow.

The UDM kids needed to do *something* before someone got hurt worse.

Willa couldn't make it rain. Her rain only worked indoors. Sebastian couldn't help, and neither could Bax or Andres.

Should Nory flux into a dritten and defend her friends?

She could if she wanted to! She could breathe fire at those Sparkies and *really* show them unsupervised flaring, if that's how they were going to act. Nory was *this close* to fluxing when she heard a loud chorus of barks. Yappy barks, menacing barks, deep barks, feverish barks.

She looked down the street. An army of dogs was running toward them. Marigold and Sebastian hopped over a fence into a nearby yard. Elliott threw himself into a bush to avoid being trampled. Nory pressed her spine to a maple tree and soaked in the scene with amazement.

Dogs, everywhere! A chocolate Lab, a Yorkshire terrier, half a dozen mutts. But not just dogs! There was also a crew of yowling cats . . . a chittering rush of squirrels and chipmunks . . . then a jackrabbit and a couple of goats. Finally, a swirl of butterflies, bluebirds, and pigeons, a rush of flapping wings.

The Sparkies screamed. They dropped their tennis balls and pivoted on their heels. Then they ran back the way they'd come. The dogs and cats and squirrels and birds, the cardinals and chipmunks and butterflies—they chased the Sparkies down the street and out of sight.

One lone tennis ball rolled into the gutter, smoking now that its flame was out.

Nory stepped away from the tree. Marigold and Sebastian joined her.

"Where did those animals come from?" Willa asked, dropping down from the tree branch she'd been clinging to. She untangled Andres's leash and pulled him behind her.

"Were they chasing the Sparkies?" Elliott

said, brushing bits of leaves off his jeans. "It looked like they were chasing the Sparkies—but that's not possible. Is it?"

Just then, Pepper ran up and stopped in the middle of the street. She flung out her arms and twirled. She was red-faced and breathing hard, and she was beaming.

"I fierced them," she cried.

"Zamboozle," said Nory.

"Amazing," said Bax.

"Nice fiercing," said Elliott. "*Really* nice."

"You rescued us!" Nory cried. "Pepper to the rescue, abracazam!"

"But where did the animals *come* from?" Willa asked.

"They were all in front of one house," Pepper said, shrugging. "On the porch. In the yard."

"I saw them," Andres said, nodding.

"Me too," Elliott said. "They took up most of the lawn. It was like a zoo—only a really sad zoo, because until Pepper went over to them, they just stood there."

"They seemed unhappy," Andres said. "Is it normal for squirrels to sit so quietly, all in a line?"

"I wonder why they were there," said Nory.

"Who knows? But as soon as Pepper showed up, they went berserk," said Elliott. "Then all she had to do was chase them in the right direction and they scared the Sparkies!"

"We win!" cried Marigold.

They all high-fived.

Andres was scratched up from the tree. Sebastian and Nory had small burns, but they weren't too bad. They decided to go back to Andres's house and eat the last of the pineapple upside-down cake. There was probably ice cream left, too, Andres said.

Nory, Bax, and Elliott walked together at the back of the group. The sky turned golden orange as the sun went down.

"I still can't figure out why those animals were in the yard," Nory said.

"Maybe some kid had a petting zoo birthday," Elliott suggested.

"With *pigeons?* Who has pigeons at a petting zoo?"

"Someone might," said Elliott. "Some people like pigeons."

"No," said Nory. "Nobody wants to pet pigeons."

Bax dug his thumbnail into his palm. He knew it wasn't a petting zoo.

It was his dad's house. *His* house.

First the ladybugs had started living on the couch. Then the gloomy chipmunk had arrived on the steps. Then, day after day, more animals had arrived. They pressed against the windows, moped on the porch, sprawled on the lawn. A couple of butterflies had made their way indoors.

They fluttered unhappily around the kitchen.

Bax didn't know why. He had asked his dad if he could use his Fuzzy magic to tell them to leave, but his dad had just shrugged. "They're not bothering anyone."

"My parents are divorced," Bax blurted. "I go back and forth between my dad and my mom. And—"

Nory stopped walking and looked at him. So did Elliott.

Bax swallowed. "That was my house. My dad's house. With all the animals."

"Oh," said Nory.

"Really?" Elliott asked. "How come?"

Bax shrugged miserably. "They're not pets or anything. They just keep showing up, and they won't go away. The goats? I hadn't even seen them yet. They must be new. I was hoping my dad would do something about them, but . . ." His voice trailed off.

"Weird," Elliott said. "Is it scary to have all those animals in your yard?"

"Not scary," said Bax. "Sad, I guess. They don't seem happy."

"Do you think they'll come back now that Pepper's not fiercing them anymore?"

Bax sighed. "From what I've seen so far? Yeah. I'd say there's a good chance."

"Do you think it's magic?" asked Elliott. "Is your dad a Fuzzy?"

They reached Andres's house. The other kids went on inside, but the three stayed outside, talking.

"Yeah," said Bax. "But he's—well, that's funny." He bit his thumb. "My dad's allergic to animal fur, but he hasn't had any problems with all these animals in our yard. No sneezing, no runny eyes, no rash, nothing. I know he trimmed the hedges this week, and watered the plants and cleaned out the garage and dug up weeds. All with the animals right there. I hadn't thought of that before."

"Your dad did all that this week?" asked Elliott. "Gosh. My dad gets like one thing done in the yard in a month."

Bax looked at Elliott. Then at Nory. "He doesn't have a job right now. So he's got a lot of time on his hands."

At first no one spoke. Nory tilted her head. Elliott pulled his eyebrows together.

Then Nory said, "I don't live with my parents at all."

Bax had met Nory's aunt Margo, but now that he thought of it, he'd never met her mom or dad. "Why not?" he asked.

"Her dad's the headmaster of Sage Academy over in Nutmeg," Elliott said. "And her mom's dead."

"Oh. I'm sorry." He looked her in the eyes when he said it. *Poor Nory.*

"My dad sent me to live with my aunt because of my upside-down magic," Nory explained, not looking away. "I guess he thought I was hard to live with. You know, just little stuff, like I set his couch on fire and chewed up his desk and squirted squid ink all over the bathroom. Also, I flunked the admissions test for his fancy school." She lifted her shoulders. "Anyway. His loss." Her tone was light, but it didn't fool Bax.

"Yeah," said Elliott. "His loss."

"I'm just saying that I know what it's like when your life doesn't turn out the way you thought it would," said Nory to Bax. She bit her lip, then did something totally unexpected. She threw herself at Bax and hugged him.

11

Your consciousness is a flame," Coach told Bax at Tuesday's tutoring session. He squatted slightly so that he was at Bax's eye level.

Bax and Nory were in Coach's office, sitting on the small couch. Coach propped his hands on his thick thighs. "Do you go camping?"

"No," Bax said. He wouldn't mind going camping. He liked the outdoors. He liked the stars. But his dad never wanted to go in the wilderness because of all the animal fur on the animals out there.

Coach looked shocked. "No? Your father

doesn't take you camping?"

Bax shook his head.

"Not your mother, either?"

"My mom does yoga and goes to book club," Bax said. "And she's a detective. My dad used to do business stuff for a museum and now he watches TV and works on the yard."

"Well, for beetroot's sake," Coach said. He scratched his head. "Can you *imagine* going camping?"

"I haven't been camping either," said Nory. "My dad's a headmaster and he reads boring books. My aunt's a taxi and she watches TV and goes to restaurants with her boyfriend. My brother plays sports and does housework, and my sister—"

"We are not talking about our family hobbies!" snapped Coach. "We are talking about camping!"

Bax looked at the floor. Nory did, too.

"Just imagine it," said Coach. "I'm trying to help you."

"Okay."

"Okay."

Coach rubbed his hands together. "So. When you go camping, you build a campfire. Right?"

Bax and Nory stared at him.

"Yes. You build a gosh-dang campfire when you go camping. Can we agree on that?"

"And sing campfire songs?" Nory asked. "I like to sing, even though my brother says I sound like a hyena?" Her eyebrows flew up. "Ooo, I wonder if I could flux into a hyena one day. I've heard they're really hard."

"Forget hyenas!" Coach said. "Forget campfire songs! I'm talking about the *fire*, people. The *fire*!" He pushed his hand over his bald head. "And when you build a fire, you *have* to *keep* the *flame* lit."

Nory blinked.

"You protect the flame," Coach went on. "You cup your hands around it. You shield it in any way you can."

"We aren't Flares," said Bax. "Our hands would get burned."

"What?"

"If we stuck them into the campfire, to protect the flame."

"It's a pretend fire. For the love of lemon juice, son, just try it!"

Bax pretended to build a campfire. He patted the air and pretended to add sticks. Nory struck imaginary matches.

Coach waved his hands about in disgust.

"No. Stop." He sighed. "That's your homework before the next time I see you, all right? Light matches. Safely. Under supervision. Light them, and keep them lit by cupping your hand around the flame. *Understand the fire*."

"Real fire?" asked Bax. Maybe his mom

could help him tonight.

"Yes, real fire. You need some experience." Coach blew his whistle. "New topic. Kittenball. I want both of you at the game this Friday at five, cheering for the team. It's the first kittenball game of the season, Dunwiddle Catnips against the Twinkle Tidbits. Did I tell you the Tidbits have a player who can flux into a kitten with six toes on each paw? Anyway. Fluxers should support their fellow Fluxers. And frankly, it's good if the older kittenballers see you UDM kids making a show of school spirit. I think that goodwill will go a long way around here. Can I count on you? Nory? Bax?"

"I'll be there," Nory said.

Bax said, "Um."

"Terrific, you can go with Nory," Coach said. "Excellent team spirit, just excellent."

On Wednesday, Nory had to walk to school alone

again, but at least this time, Elliott called the night before to say he wasn't coming. "I have a thing to do," he'd said mysteriously.

Nory was a little hurt. Elliott was her best friend at school. So why was he keeping secrets from her?

She left the house early to avoid the Sparkies, and when she arrived at school, Paige from kittenball was waiting for her near the front door. Akari and Finn were with her.

Nory spotted Bax a few yards behind them. He was here unusually early, she thought. He was sitting on the floor with his back to his locker, reading a paperback. She thought about calling him over, but Paige looped her arm in Nory's.

"Do you want to come to the store with us before practice?" Paige asked. "We decided we need chocolate to erase the taste of pomegranate juice and seaweed."

Nory glowed. "Yeah. Absolutely."

"Great," said Paige. "Meet us back here at three o'clock."

Nory grinned. She had kittenball friends. They were inviting her to go buy candy! Abracazam!

From the opposite side of the hall came a scream.

Who, what, where?

It was Lacey Clench.

Her hand was on her open locker, and rocks were tumbling out, landing around her. On her. The floor shook with the clatter.

Nory's heart stopped.

Rocks? More rocks? Why?

"What the zum-zum?" Lacey yelled. She stomped her foot. "Who turned my stuff to stone?!"

Kids stepped closer. Akari walked over, knelt, and hefted up a large gray rock, which he held high so everyone could see.

"It's shaped like a notebook!" he called. "That is so cool!"

Nory was worried. Lacey would blame this on UDM.

"This one's a pencil," said Paige, picking up a pencil-shaped piece of quartz. To Lacey, she said, "It's really pretty."

Lacey snatched it back. "It's a *stone*! My math book is a *stone*! My English journal is—"

"A stone?" Akari asked. He and Finn laughed.

"Shut up," Lacey snapped. She spotted Nory and scowled. "You!" she said, pointing. "You did this, Nory Horace. You and your wonky friends!"

"No!" Nory said. "I swear!"

"I know you did," said Lacey. "You Flops are up to something! You were spying on us this weekend!"

"Yeah, and you threw flaming tennis balls at us," said Nory. "But I did not turn the stuff in your locker to stone. I'm a Fluxer, Lacey. I couldn't even do it if I wanted to."

"My dad is going to be so mad!" Lacey barked. "This is the work of upside-down magic *for sure*."

"Calm down, Lacey," Zinnia said. "I'll loan you whatever you need, all right?"

She opened her locker, which was three down from Lacey's, and cried out. Her school supplies had been turned into rocks, too. "Zowie!"

Rune opened his locker, and same thing: A spiral notebook made of granite slid out and landed on his toe. "Ow!"

"They're out to get us," Lacey said to her friends. "Don't you see? First the Flops spied on us, and now they're ruining our stuff!"

"We are not out to get you!" Nory said. "You're out to get *us*! You're trying to get us to do messed-up magic so we get in trouble! In fact—oh, zamboozle! Did *you* replace your own books with fake rocks? To make it look like we don't belong in school?"

But Lacey wasn't responsible. She couldn't be, because as students arrived for the day, more and more stones spilled from more and more lockers. Stones shaped like books. Stones shaped like pencils, and rocks shaped like pencil cases. Stones shaped like locker mirrors and packs of gum and hairbrushes. There was no way Lacey could have pulled off a prank this massive.

Bax, though. Nory felt like a traitor just for thinking it, but Bax had been at school when Nory arrived. What if he got here early for a reason? A rock reason?

She searched for him. He wasn't sitting on the floor and reading anymore. He'd gotten to his feet, and she watched as he twisted the dial on his locker. He opened the door, and a landslide of rocks poured out.

No. It couldn't be Bax, then. He would never turn his own things to stone.

Two lockers down, the same thing happened to Marigold.

Principal Gonzalez waded through the crowd. "Please keep calm," he called. "Go to your classes. Your studies are more important than these rocks!"

"But who's going to get in trouble?" Lacey whined. "And who's going to make everything normal?"

Paige glanced at Nory. "I know you didn't do this, but it looks pretty bad."

"Why?"

"You just said Lacey and those Sparkie guys threw flaming tennis balls at you. Now she and her friends have their stuff ruined."

"But Bax's stuff was ruined, too," Nory said. "So was Marigold's!"

"I know," Paige said. "Just, other people might think you did that on purpose so that you wouldn't look suspicious. Plus, that one friend of yours can turn into a rock for real." Paige shifted uncomfortably. "People might wonder, that's all."

Ms. Starr made them do another trust exercise. This one meant finding a partner and falling backward, trusting the other person to catch you. Willa was partnered with Elliott, Nory with Marigold, and Bax with Pepper. Andres couldn't do it. Sebastian had to partner with Ms. Starr.

Bax caught Pepper just fine, but when it was Pepper's turn to catch him, he couldn't make himself fall backward. He felt awkward and he nearly fluxed. Still, he managed to calm himself down and stay human.

"Don't worry," Pepper told him. "Do you want to try it again?"

Bax watched Marigold almost drop Nory.

"Oops," Marigold cried, clutching Nory by her armpits. "I panicked. I didn't want to shrink you."

"Now," said Ms. Starr, gesturing for them to

return to their desks. "In an atmosphere of trust, let's talk about what happened with the lockers today."

"It wasn't me!" Bax said, flushing.

"No one said it was," said Ms. Starr.

"But you're thinking it. You all are. I can tell!"

"Did you maybe do it and then forget?" Marigold asked.

"Do you ever shrink things and then forget?" Bax asked.

Marigold looked ashamed. "No. Sorry."

"You *were* at school early," Sebastian said.

"He had rocks in his locker, too, though!" Nory said.

Bax tensed his jaw. "I only got here early because I spend Tuesday nights at my mom's house. She drove me to school today." He swallowed. "But Andres was here before I was."

Andres shrugged. "Carmen had a project she

needed to work on. She made us get here an entire hour early."

"And you," Nory said, pointing at Elliott. "You said you had 'a thing to do.' But you wouldn't say what it was. Where were you? Don't say it was tutoring, because you don't have tutoring on Wednesdays."

Everyone stared at Elliott.

He turned red. "I was working with Willa."

"On what?" Marigold asked.

"Yeah," said Nory. "On what?"

"We can't tell," Willa said, a small smile on her face.

Nory didn't really suspect Elliott. He was too nice a person to turn people's stuff to rocks. And his magic wouldn't let him do it, anyway. Would it? But she wished she could wipe that smile off Willa's face. And she wished Elliott would stop keeping secrets.

"Let's move on," Ms. Starr said. "It doesn't

matter who was here early, because no one in this class was responsible for what happened with the lockers. I know that none of you were responsible. All right, kids?"

She gave them a hard look, as if to drill into each and every one of their minds that she believed in them. Nory's chest loosened. The atmosphere in the entire room loosened.

"Still, people are talking and rumors are flying. It's no fun to be on the receiving end of unkind behavior," Ms. Starr said. "Let's brainstorm together some appropriate ways to handle mean remarks."

Bax had an idea. "What if Lacey did it herself? Or together with the Sparkies?"

"Why would she turn her own stuff to stone?" Marigold said.

"To set us up. To make it look like it was us," said Bax.

"I thought of that," Nory said. "But how

would they get rocks shaped liked books? Do you think they could have actually flared stuff into rocks?"

"Class!" said Ms. Starr. "Our goal is to work through the rumors and unkindness in a positive way, but you keep playing the blame game. How does that help anyone?"

Everyone fell silent. Bax felt sorry.

Ms. Starr blew out a sigh. "Tell you what. Let's stop discussing this for a bit and instead practice our headstands. Seeing the world from an upside-down perspective always helps us, one way or another."

The class set a new record: Every single kid held their headstand for a full two minutes.

Bax didn't actually do headstands, because whenever he tried, he turned into a rock. He and Ms. Starr had figured out an alternative where he leaned backward over the seat of a chair, and got his head upside-down that way.

Two minutes was a long time, but when he came up, he had to admit that he felt better.

12

At three o'clock, Nory waited for her kittenball teammates at the front of the school. They were going to the candy store.

Only Paige showed up.

"Sorry," said Paige. "It's just us. The boys wouldn't come."

"Why not?"

"You know, the locker thing. With the rocks. Finn is upset, and Akari pretty much does what Finn does."

They headed in the direction of the high school. Two blocks away, there was a little row of shops: a pizzeria, a newsstand, a stationery store, and a corner shop that had fruit and groceries and candy.

"Finn thought the rocks in the lockers were funny," Nory said. "Why is he mad now?"

"He thought it was funny when it happened to Lacey. When he found out his own stuff was turned to stone—not so much. His phone turned into a rock, and his parents had told him they wouldn't replace it if it got broken. His baseball cards were ruined, too, and the scarf his sister knitted."

"Okay. But he knows *I* didn't do it, right?" said Nory.

Paige's eyes slid away. They reached the shop and stood outside the entrance. "I think so. But nothing like this happened until this year, when the Upside-Down Magic class was offered for the first time."

"Don't you believe me?" Nory asked.

Paige pressed the heels of her palms over her eyes. Then she dropped her hands. "I want to," she said. "We all do. But somebody played that joke, and it wasn't funny, and people are saying that if all of the UDM kids worked together, you could have managed it."

"We could *not* have managed it!" Nory yelled.

"Then give me a better explanation!" Paige said.

Nory couldn't.

Neither girl spoke. Nory tried not to scream, she was so frustrated. Finally, Paige went inside the store.

When she came back out, she silently handed Nory a chocolate bar, but she didn't talk to her for the entire kittenball practice, when other people were around.

At tutoring the next day, Bax was glad to be able to tell Coach he'd done his fire homework. Twice.

"My aunt wouldn't let me do it," said Nory.

"My mom and I did it on Tuesday," Bax said. His mom had lit an aromatherapy candle and he had studied the flame while she tried to get him to do yoga poses. "And my dad and I did it again last night." They'd dimmed the lights and lit matches over the kitchen counter, cupping their hands around the flames to help them stay lit. Both nights had been surprisingly fun.

"All right, then," said Coach. "Excellent. Now what you want to do is think of your spirit— the part of you that makes you *you*—as a flame. You want to keep it lit. Keep the flame alive. Protect it. If you work on that, then you'll gradually learn to keep your spirit alert when you're a rock."

"I'll try," Bax said.

"I learned this technique when I studied reptile fluxing in college," said Coach. "Reptiles are cold-blooded. Turtles and crocodiles are somewhat rocklike themselves, aren't they? They spend a lot of time just sitting around. In a cold-blooded body, it's easy to lose track of your human flame. Reptile Fluxers learn this flame technique, so I figured it was worth a shot with you."

Bax thought about the flame.

He thought about keeping it lit.

He thought about protecting it, inside his mind.

"Okay, flux!" yelled Coach.

Bax's face dried up. That's what it felt like. Then his legs folded in. Stiffness moved from his feet to his head, and a gluey thickness stilled his blood and breath.

But he held the flame, the flame that was his spirit.

He was doing it! He was a rock *but he was still Bax*!

"Did you see that?" Coach asked. "Amazing!"

"Is he still Bax?" Nory asked. "I mean, of course he's Bax. But does he know he's Bax?"

"Bax! Hello!" yelled Coach. "Can you hear us?"

Bax couldn't answer. But he *could* hear.

It was amazing.

This had never, ever happened before.

He was Rock-Bax. He felt like rolling over and bouncing.

But he couldn't.

He felt like singing.

But he couldn't.

Okay. He still couldn't do anything physical. But he could *hear*. And he could *think*.

"Hmmm. Another tricky part, huh? If he *can* hear us"—*I can!* thought Bax—"how would he let us know?" Coach sighed. "I'll take him to the nurse's office. Nory, you go back to class."

Bax heard humming. Beautiful humming. He heard the faint crush of carpet fibers, and the creak of wood. Wonderful noises! Then grunting, awesome grunting, as Coach lifted Rock-Bax up and dropped him into the wheelbarrow. He could hear. He could hear!

Hallway sounds filtered in: the bang of lockers, the chatter of kids, the echo of footfalls.

"Happened again, hmm?" Rock-Bax heard a man say. It was Principal Gonzalez. Bax recognized the deep voice.

The wheelbarrow stopped moving. "Oh, we're making progress!" Coach replied. "Fluxing more on purpose, less by accident. And he did his homework. I just don't know if the new technique I taught him worked yet."

Principal Gonzalez made a sound of displeasure. "Filling lockers with rocks is not the kind of progress I was hoping for."

"That wasn't Bax," said Coach. "Fluxing doesn't work that way."

"His might."

"He said it wasn't him," Coach persisted. "And I'm certainly not comfortable calling him a liar. Are you?"

"I suppose not." The principal sighed. "But he's not the happiest of boys, and he has this rock talent. There's no question that whoever's doing these pranks has upside-down magic. I've investigated every other possibility and can't come up with anything."

"Bax is a good kid," said Coach. "He wouldn't ruin all those coats and notebooks. Ms. Starr's program is helping him. It's helping all those kids."

Coach started pushing the wheelbarrow again. As Bax was bumped down the hall, he focused on keeping his flame lit inside his rock shape. The flame was him. It was his mind and heart and sense of humor; it was his excitement at tigerball and the books by his bedside at night; it was the way he felt when he laughed or cried.

He was sad the principal suspected him, but nonetheless he felt a warm little stony glow. Coach believed in him. He really did.

Nurse Riley painted on the Burtlebox, and for the first time ever, Bax felt himself flux back into a boy. It felt good. Like getting out of a cramped car and being able to stretch your legs.

"Did you keep the flame, son?" asked Coach.

Bax nodded.

"Milestone! Oops. I mean, rock on! Oh, drat. For the love of seaweed, I mean—" Coach high-fived Bax.

"What did he do?" Nurse Riley's eyebrows went up.

"Tell him, son!" Coach was beaming.

"I kept my human mind," said Bax softly.

"What?" Nurse Riley clapped him on the back. "Get out. You did *not*," he joked.

"I did," said Bax.

"He did," said Coach.

Nurse Riley jumped up and down. "The human mind! In a rock! You are so awesome, Bax. I couldn't be happier."

He held up a waiting hand and rushed into the back room. He returned with three tiny bottles of ginger ale. "We have this stuff to stop people from yakking if they're nauseated," he said.

Coach shook his head. "You should give plain yogurt to your yakkers, if you want my two cents. Plain yogurt and papaya."

"Good to know," Nurse Riley said. He handed out the ginger ale. "A toast. To Bax!"

"To Bax," they cheered.

The tops of the bottles made hissing sounds as they came off.

Back in class, Nory waggled her eyebrows at Bax.

Bax got out his food diary and wrote *ginger ale.*

Nory waved at Bax while Ms. Starr was writing math problems on the board. "How did it go?"

Bax got out his ruler and pencil.

"Bax!" whispered Nory.

"What?"

"You know what!"

Bax made a face like, *I have no idea what you're talking about.*

Ms. Starr was still writing problems on the board.

Nory fluxed into a kitten and leapt from her own chair to Bax's desk. She put her Kitten-Nory face in his and opened her eyes wide.

"Okay, fine," he whispered. "I did it. I kept my human mind." His face broke out in a huge grin.

Kitten-Nory did a little kitten jig and then chased her tail in the center of Bax's desk.

"Please keep human form during math class," said Ms. Starr, without even turning around.

13

The next day, Nory ate lunch with Bax and Pepper. It was tacos. Nory had hers with extra cheese and tomatoes. Pepper had shredded lettuce. Bax had the works.

"So I was thinking after school we could all go for pizza and then to the kittenball game," Nory told Pepper. "Coach says it's a good idea for the UDM kids to go to school events. To cheer and show school spirit and all that. Be part of the community."

Pepper hesitated.

"I'm going," said Bax. He actually sounded

cheery about it, Nory thought.

"We're all going," she told Pepper. "Even Sebastian, though he might have to wear his blindfold."

"I can come for pizza, but not the game," said Pepper softly.

"Family stuff?"

She shook her head. "I'd fierce the kittens. You know I can't turn my magic off."

Oh. Nory hadn't thought of that. Pepper couldn't go to farms, or aquariums, or kittenball games. Not now, and not ever, unless her upside-down magic got under control.

"I wish I could come," said Pepper. "Cheer for me, 'kay?" She looked down at her plate and began eating as if there was nothing more to be said on the matter.

They ate tacos in silence for a minute, and then Nory looked up. Oh, zamboozle. There was Lacey Clench, talking to the kids from beginner kittenball. Her body went rigid.

"I hear Lacey's telling people that if she gets the full fifty signatures, Principal Gonzalez will have to remove our program," Pepper told Nory.

"When I was a rock," Bax told them, "I heard the principal say he thought the pranks were done by a UDM student."

Nory's stomach twisted.

"Really?" asked Pepper. "If the principal is against our class, we're doomed."

Nory tried to look on the bright side. "I bet Lacey won't get fifty signatures. There can't be that many mean people at our school."

"A ton of people with lockers in my row signed it," Bax said.

"Could we steal the petition?" Nory asked. "Or could Marigold shrink it down to nothing?"

Pepper shook her head. "That's not right. Also, they'd know it was us."

"Then I'm going to do something, right now,"

said Nory. She stood and walked over to the table where Lacey stood, holding the petition clutched against her chest. "Paige?" Nory said. "Akari? Finn?"

Paige's eyes grew huge.

"Are you signing Lacey's petition?" Nory asked.

Finn kicked at the floor and dropped his eyes.

Lacey waggled the petition at him. "Sign it now, if you want to join the others," she said. "Or go off and be friends with the wonko. I don't care. There are lots of other people I can ask. Sixth graders. Seventh graders!"

Nory felt the urge to flux. Maybe a skunkephant. Or a dritten. She could make that Lacey Clench run away in fear. She had done it before, and she could do it again.

But no.

Fluxing in the cafeteria had never solved any problems. She took a deep breath, the way

Ms. Starr had taught her.

She did not flux.

Instead, she spoke loud and strong. "The kids in the Upside-Down Magic class are kids just like you, Lacey. We eat the same tacos, we drink the same chocolate milk, we have friends, we do homework, we play sports. Yeah, it's not always easy to have us in school. I get that."

"That mitten was scary," said Akari.

"And Marigold shrank me!" said Lacey.

"Sure, but Flares have flaring accidents, and Flickers have flickering accidents, and Fluxers learning carnivores can be scary, too. The lockers have gone invisible before. The library caught fire. We're just used to those things, because they happen all the time. We call a teacher, or use a fire extinguisher, and then we go on with our day."

Lacey crossed her arms and scowled.

"Lacey," Nory went on, "do you really and

truly know, without a doubt, that my friends and I are to blame for turning the things in the lockers to stone?"

"Yes."

"Do you have proof?"

"I don't need to prove what everyone knows already, Nory Horace."

"Lacey, I think you should leave Nory alone now," said Paige. She got up from the table and stood beside Nory.

"I'm not bothering her," said Lacey. "She's bothering me."

"Please. Just walk away," said Paige. She took Nory's hand and squeezed.

Akari got up.

Finn got up, too.

Nory's heart swelled. She took in the faces of her kittenball friends, and looked around at Pepper and others, who were staring at them.

"We don't have to fight, Lacey," Nory said.

"We can all be better, don't you think?"

Lacey Clench rolled her eyes and stomped out of the cafeteria.

14

The UDM kids met up after school at the pizzeria by the corner store. All eight kids squeezed into one booth. They were squished, but together. They ordered pizza.

Nory was happy. She liked that she got to be next to Elliott, and he was being fun instead of secretive. He froze her lemonade into a slushie when the waiter wasn't looking.

"Sebastian, scooch over," said Marigold. She was squashed between Sebastian and Andres.

"Don't scooch," said Bax, who was on Sebastian's other side. "You're already poking me with the dog cone you're wearing."

Sebastian's hand went to the white plastic cone around his head. It looked like one of the contraptions dogs wore when recovering from surgeries, because that's exactly what it was. Nory knew because she'd read the price sticker, which Sebastian had forgotten to peel off. It read: DOG CONE, XXL, $7.99. PET VILLAGE.

Sebastian swung the cone around so his face could look at Bax. "It's a *head* cone," he said, "since I wear it around my *head*."

Bax cocked his eyebrow. "Dogs wear them around their heads."

"But I'm not a dog," Sebastian said. He lifted his chin. "I'm a human."

Nory turned to Sebastian. "Do you have to wear it while you eat?"

"Today's my first day to try it," Sebastian said. "I have to get used to it, like people do with glasses."

"You don't have to get used to glasses, actually," Pepper said.

Sebastian twisted toward her. As he moved, his cone tipped over a shaker of Parmesan cheese.

"Pepper's right," Marigold said. She tapped her own ear. "You shouldn't have to get used to it. With my hearing aid, I turn it on, and it works."

Sebastian swung his head the other way to look at Marigold, since the cone didn't allow him any peripheral vision. "My head cone is an *experiment*," he said. "I'm working on my upside-down magic by thinking outside of the box, like Ms. Starr said."

"Out of the box and into the cone," Bax said.

Sebastian whipped around, and his cone whacked Bax's cheek.

"*Ow*," Bax said. "Seriously, dude? You can't just take it off for ten minutes?"

Sebastian exhaled. "The cone blocks sound waves that come in from the sides, so I don't get distracted. Think of how a horse wears blinders so that he only focuses on what's in front of him. This is the same thing, but with sound. If it works, I am thinking I could wear it in superloud situations, instead of my blindfold."

"Andres, since Sebastian won't take off his cone, would you mind going up to the ceiling?" Marigold asked. "Then we can spread out, and you'll be more comfortable, too." Marigold was squashed between Sebastian and Andres, who was wearing a backpack of bricks and was held down by a web of bungee cords looped around his chair and threaded through the table legs.

Andres grabbed the napkin dispenser as if it might help weigh him down. "Go up to the ceiling in front of strangers? No way!"

"What are you going to do at the kittenball game?" Pepper asked. "The arena has bleacher seats."

Andres paled. His gaze went far off, as if

imagining himself floating above the slick, flat benches, his leash and his bungee cords dangling from him like streamers.

"We can get more bricks for his backpack," Nory said. But she felt her stomach squeeze. She hadn't really thought about Andres at the game.

"Then it'll be too heavy for anyone to carry over there," Andres said, shaking his head. "Maybe I should stay home."

Nory's heart sank.

"Sebastian?" Marigold said. "What about your head cone? Are you wearing that to the game?"

"I am *committed* to my head cone," Sebastian said. "What don't you understand about that?"

Elliott put down his pizza crust. "Nory, maybe all of us going to the kittenball game isn't such a great plan."

"No!" Nory cried. She clapped her hand over her mouth. She had never spoken so sharply to him before. "I mean . . . I mean . . ."

"The Sparkies are already out to get us," Marigold said flatly. "If we show up with a dog cone—"

"*Head* cone!"

"—and bungee cords and bricks . . ." She ripped her napkin in half, then in half again. "It's a nice idea, all of us sticking together, but something's going to go wrong."

"Come on," Nory said. "We'll be showing school spirit, which will help prove we're no different than anyone else at Dunwiddle."

"Except we *are* different," said Marigold. Her gaze flicked to Sebastian, and then to Andres. She stared at her napkin. "Everyone can see it, and we might do some damage. What if I shrink someone?"

"Marigold's right," Elliott said. "It's too risky."

Nory turned a pleading gaze on Pepper, then remembered that Pepper had already said she wouldn't be attending the game—and for good reason. She would fierce the kittenball players.

Were the others' reasons just as good?

No.

Maybe.

"Coach says a team is only as strong as its weakest player," Nory said, hating the wobble in her voice.

"Well, I'm the weakest, then," said Andres, loosening his cord and sliding carefully out of the booth, holding on to the table as his feet floated a couple of inches off the floor. "And I'm sorry, but I'm going home."

Elliott slapped money on the table. He squirmed past Nory and out of the booth, then took hold of Andres's leash.

Marigold put money down, too. "Mr. Vitomin is your coach, not mine," she told Nory. "And I don't think I'm being weak. I think I'm being smart."

In the end, only Bax, Nory, Sebastian, and Willa went to the game. The kittenball arena was only a couple of blocks from school and the pizzeria. The high school used it, too. It was bigger than Bax had imagined, given that the actual kitten-ball field was only the size of a living room. Lots of people brought binoculars.

Older Flyers zoomed and zipped across the top of the arena, trailing school banners. "Milk! Tuna!" Fuzzies yelled, holding out cat treats at the edge of the field. Part of kittenball tradition was that Fuzzies clustered on the sidelines, try-ing to distract the players of the opposing teams. Laser pointers had been banned. So far today, the players had kept their human minds and hadn't been tempted by the Fuzzy magic.

"Oh, zum-zum," Nory muttered, nudging Bax with her elbow. She jerked her head.

Ugh. The Sparkies were sitting down next to

them. Bax saw Lacey, Rune, and Zinnia, plus their recruits from the tree house. Lacey had her petition with her.

"You'd think she'd give it a rest," Nory whispered into Bax's ear.

"She'll never give anything a rest," said Bax. "She is not a restful girl."

"They must be plotting something. They wouldn't sit by us if they weren't," said Sebastian. He was wearing his head cone and had to turn his whole body every time he wanted to see anything.

Nory clenched her hands into fists and leaned forward. "How come you're here?" she asked Lacey directly.

"To cheer on our kittenball team," Lacey said sweetly. "Why else?"

"Right," said Willa. "I highly doubt that."

No grown-ups were around, but Lacey lowered her voice anyway. "We're going to flush you out. Won't that be fun?"

"Sit back," Bax said to Nory under his breath. "Don't let her get to you. That's exactly what she wants."

"Everyone is here at the kittenball game," said Lacey, as falsely pleasant as ever. "The fluxing teachers from all the grades. The principal, the vice principal. Ooh, I can even see the guidance counselor, two Flare teachers, a Flyer teacher, and two lunch-duty ladies. There are some high schoolers here, too, and loads of parents. I sure hope nothing wonky happens at this kittenball game! Because if it does, *every single person will see who's to blame.*"

Bax thought about the spying day, on Andres's birthday. He should have realized the Sparkies would try something like this. Here, where parents and school administration would all see. Marigold was right.

"Nory," Bax said. "Let's move to a different

part of the arena."

"No way," Nory said. "These are really good seats. If we move we'll be way in the back. We can't let them scare us."

Lacey waved her petition. "We'll get more signatures than we need, and Principal Gonzalez will have to listen to us. You'll see."

Below on the field, the referee spoke into a microphone. She wore a leopard-print shirt. "Welcome to the Twinkle Tidbits versus the Dunwiddle Catnips! Let the middle school kittenball season officially BEGIN!"

The crowd cheered.

Sebastian grimaced. "Oh, ow, the visible sound waves. My head cone is not going to be enough if everyone is cheering and shouting into that microphone." He took his head cone off, unlatching a clip at his neck and setting it on the floor by his feet. "I'm going to have to switch to the blindfold. Wait. Wait. Where's my blindfold?" he asked, patting his pockets.

The crowd started yelling.

Who's gonna pounce? CatNIPs CatNIPs
And who's gonna rule? CatNIPs CatNIPs
We swat so sweet, admit defeat!
You cannot beat
our Catnip!

"Have you seen my blindfold?" Sebastian asked his friends. "It was in my back pocket but now I can't find it. My eyes are really hurting with this cheer." Nory and Willa started looking around on the floor of the bleachers. No luck.

Oh!

Bax spotted the blindfold in Rune's hands. Rune must have pickpocketed Sebastian! Now he was shoving the blindfold into his backpack. When he pulled his hand back out, he held a pair of maracas.

"Have a look at these sound waves, wonko!" Rune cried, switching one of the maracas to his other hand and banging them together. Sebastian hunched down, overwhelmed. Zinnia got out a triangle and jangled it around. Lacey shook a set of jingle bells. Sebastian covered his eyes and let out a low moan. He needed his cone or his blindfold, but he wasn't wearing either.

People started to stare.

Then a whistle blew, and everyone turned their attention to the kittenball field. The kittens faced off. Their spines arched. Their tails quivered. The Dunwiddle Catnips wore bright red collars. The Twinkle Tidbits wore yellow.

"Here, kitty, kitty!" the referee cried. She tossed the red yarnball high.

Fur flew. The kittens pounced and rolled, darted and dodged. They swatted the ball and tail-whacked. One of the Dunwiddle kittens pounced on a Twinkle calico, and the calico fluxed into a dazed twelve-year-old girl.

"Out!" the referee yelled, pointing at the girl. She pointed next at the Dunwiddle kitten. "And you, watch those claws! One foot of yarn penalty!"

A new kitten went in for Twinkle, too—it was the six-toed wonder. Wow, that kitty could swat the ball. Bax got a kick out of watching Nory, who leaned forward with bright eyes. There was an amazing whack! And a pounce! Now the yellow yarnball was in play and Dunwiddle was fighting back with a paw kick that sent the yarn unrolling across the playing field. Go, Catnips! Go, Catnips!

Bax got caught up in the game, too. Until he heard the singing.

"Rain, rain, go away, come again another day!"

It was the Sparkies. They had surrounded Willa and Sebastian. They were singing and singing, banging their instruments. They splashed Willa with water from a water bottle. "Rain, rain, go away!"

Willa blinked rapidly. Her cheeks grew pink. She tried to scoot away, but the Sparkies leaned in closer. Sebastian was still rocking with his eyes shut.

"Stop it!" Bax yelled. "Leave them alone!"

"Rain, rain, go away! Come again another day!" the Sparkies sang.

"Don't rain, Willa!" Nory interrupted. "Don't give them the satisfaction."

But the Sparkies kept singing.

And Sebastian kept rocking.

Willa covered her ears.

Bax's chest tightened. Then the skin of his face tightened. Then his bones tingled in a way he recognized, and he went from helpless to terrified.

No, he told himself. *Do not flux.*

He flattened his hands on the bench. *Deep breath. Hold the flame, just in case, but do. Not. Flux.*

Oh, no. Oh, wow. He hadn't fluxed, but the stadium bench, on which he was pressing down, changed from ridged plastic to hard gray limestone.

Bax jerked his hands away, but the shift of bench into stone continued, moving out from where Bax's hands had been.

It turned to stone under Willa. And Sebastian. And everyone beyond.

The floor beneath their feet changed, too! The wood became granite, and everything *on* the floor turned into rock. Backpacks, jackets, drink cups. Nothing changed that was connected to people, but belongings that weren't—cameras, phones, purses—all turned to stone. The transformation rippled through the arena.

It was as clear as sunlight to Bax that

he was responsible.

He had started this. He hadn't meant to do it—but he, Bax, was guilty.

"Nory!" Bax called out. "Nory, I have to get out of here!"

His words were swallowed by the rising tide of confusion. Toddlers wailed when their stuffed animals went from soft to hard. People's drinks turned to concrete. A flurry of voices rang out.

"What's happening?"

"My purse!"

"My coat!"

"The car keys are in there."

"My money is in there."

Bax jumped to his feet. He tugged on Nory. She turned to him.

"It's me!" Bax said.

"What?"

He had to yell. "It's me! I started it, and it's rippling out. I'm the one turning things to rocks!"

Nory's face looked so shocked that Bax stopped breathing.

Then he made himself inhale. He pushed through the crowd. He reached the parking lot and started to run.

15

Nory took off after Bax.

She ran across the stone floor of the bleach-ers, down the stone steps, and pushed through the heavy stone doors. She saw Bax ahead of her, running down the sidewalk. She called his name, but he didn't stop.

It was ten blocks to Bax's dad's home. Nory followed him all the way there, running.

She caught up with him outside the house. He had stopped, finally, and was sitting on the porch with his head bowed. Next to him was a mourn-ful-looking basset hound. Next to the basset hound were two lethargic squirrels. Nory also spotted two goats, several mutts, a German shepherd, some bluebirds, a ton of pigeons, and a teacup pig, all lying on the lawn. There were clusters of chipmunks leaning against the front windowsills. From the backyard came a low, grumbling, snorting moan, and a thread of fear snaked up Nory's spine.

Something very large was making that moan. Something very large and very unhappy.

"It's a rhino," Bax said without lifting his head. "It arrived this morning."

Nory sat down next to him. "Why? How? Where did it come from?"

"I have no idea," Bax said. "Just like I have no idea how I . . . you know. Turned everything into stone at the kittenball game." His voice caught. "I didn't mean to, Nory, I swear I didn't. I didn't even know I was doing it until I looked down. It was all spreading from me!"

Nory was shocked. "Did you do the pennies, too?"

Bax shrugged miserably. "I guess I must have. But not on purpose, and I didn't even know. I brought a pocketful of coins in for the Pennies for Potions jar that morning, and that must have been the start of it. It spreads out from something I touch, I guess? It doesn't happen all at once."

"And the stuff inside the lockers?"

"I must have done that, too. I came to school early that day. I had—I had had an argument with my mom about my dad. I was pretty upset. Maybe that had something to do with it. It must have started from something I touched in my locker, and spread from there."

"Has it happened before?" Nory asked.

"Before what?"

"Before the pennies. Were there other times when you turned something other than yourself to stone?"

"I don't think so. But I don't know," Bax moaned.

They needed a grown-up. "We should tell your dad," Nory said. "Let's go inside."

"I'm not sure," said Bax. "My dad has enough to worry about."

"We have to," said Nory. "Come on." She got to her feet and opened the front door. "Hello! Mr. Kapoor?"

"He's probably watching TV," Bax said. "Watch out for ladybugs. They're kind of every-where." They went into the living room. In the corner stood a piano. There was dust on the frame, but not the keys. In the middle of the room was a TV, also dusty, with a couch in front of it. On the couch sat a man with slumped shoulders.

"Hey, Dad," Bax said. "This is my friend Nory. Nory, this is my dad."

Mr. Kapoor switched off the TV and turned to face them. Nory took him in.

He looked like Bax, with high cheekbones and warm brown skin, but his eyes had bags beneath them. Kind, sad eyes. "Bax," he said. "I thought the game wasn't over till six. How come you're home early?"

"Mr. Kapoor?" Nory said. "Nice to meet you."

"Nice to meet you, too."

"Bax hasn't been feeling well," said Nory. "Something's new with his magic and it's pretty scary."

Mr. Kapoor squinted. "What do you mean? The Burtlebox always works. It's still working for you, right, Bax?"

"Yes," Bax said. "This is something different. I'm turning things to stone, Dad. Other things. That aren't me. I can't control it. "

Mr. Kapoor shook his head, then exhaled deeply and sank back into the couch. "Wow," he said. "I never heard of anything like that."

"We need help," said Nory.

"I'm not sure what to do," Mr. Kapoor said. He didn't get up. "Maybe you should take some more medicine, Bax?"

Bax sighed. "I don't think that's going to help. The whole kittenball arena turned to stone. Taking more Burtlebox isn't going to turn it back."

Poor Bax. He had to take that Burtlebox all the time. Every day.

Oh. Zamboozle! Nory had an idea. She clutched Bax's arm. "Do you remember what Nurse Riley said?"

Bax shook his head.

"He said, *With these individual potions, you don't always know how a person's body will react with long-term use.*"

"So?"

"So maybe you're taking too much potion and

186

it's messing up your fluxing!" cried Nory.

"But the potion *helps* me," said Bax.

"It changes you back, yes, but maybe it has side effects!"

"The potion is making me turn things to stone?"

"Maybe. Maybe you take so much of it you get a side effect. I don't know. We have to talk to a doctor."

"The animals around the house—could that be because of my medicine, too?" Bax wondered.

Nory thought for a minute. "I don't see how. But hey! What if I fluxed into a kitten? Maybe I could get a sense of what's going on with the animals!"

"Would you try?"

Nory concentrated hard and fluxed. *Pop! Pop!* The colors around her grew muted, as they always did when she was Kitten-Nory. Far-off objects grew fuzzy, since cats had poor long-distance vision. Smells grew stronger. She tried to keep control of her human mind, but suddenly— she wanted to lie down.

She felt sad.

She didn't know why.

She padded toward the living room, and to Bax's dad on the couch.

There was something about Mr. Kapoor. It was like he was pulling her toward him with his unhappiness.

Stop! Danger! Nory's human mind said.

But Kitten-Nory's mind sank into sadness. Nothing mattered. Everything was gray. Moving was a struggle, so she dropped where she was, at Mr. Kapoor's feet.

"Get out!" Girl-Nory said to herself. *"Flux back!"*

Why bother? Kitten-Nory thought. Then Kitten-Nory stopped thinking. Stopped thinking, stopped caring. Nothing mattered. The world was bleak, had always been bleak, would always be bleak. Why fight it?

Hands lifted her up. Boy eyes met her kitten eyes.

"Nory!" the boy barked.

Bax? her human mind thought.

"Nory. Flux back. You have to flux back, now!"

And with a huge effort, Nory did.

"Whoa," she said, a girl again.

She ran over to Bax's dad. "Mr. Kapoor?"

"Oh . . . ah, yes?"

"Something kind of weird just happened, and I was wondering . . ." She swallowed. "Do you have upside-down magic?"

Mr. Kapoor looked scared. His gaze flicked to Bax, then to Nory. Then he stared at his laptop and nodded.

"And when animals get near you, they get

sad," said Nory. "That's what happened to me, just now, when I fluxed into a kitten. That's why all these animals are around your house. You're pulling them in and making them unhappy."

"I wondered if that was the case," Bax's dad murmured.

"You're an Upside-Down Fuzzy?" Bax said to his dad. "I thought you were an allergic Fuzzy."

"I'm so sorry, Bax. I should have told you. I was ashamed of my magic, and then when I learned about you and your magic, and you started going to this new program, I got ashamed of being ashamed."

Bax's dad had known about his magic since he was ten, he told them. He explained that animals took on his emotions, whether good *or* bad. Sometimes he made them happy, and that was nice. Sometimes he made them nervous, or jealous, or sad. But back when Bax's dad was young, people didn't call wonky magic "upside down" and they didn't have educational programs to help with it. All his friends thought his upside-down magic was scary and weird, so he had hated it, too. When he moved to a new town, he had started telling people he was allergic to animals, and resolved never to talk about his magic.

"I should have told you, Bax," he said again. "I should have told your mother. I was just ashamed of being upside-down. And then I heard about the new class at Dunwiddle and I was so glad there was a chance for you to have a different experience."

Bax regarded his dad. He was a kind man. And so sad. About his upside-down magic, about his divorce, about losing his job.

I will tell Ms. Starr, Bax thought. Ms. Starr, who wore bright clothes and matching sneakers. Who believed in headstands and Hula-Hoops and trust exercises. Who taught her students to understand their feelings deeply, rather than control them.

He would tell her right away, and explain everything, because if anyone could help Dad, it was Ms. Starr.

"Look," Nory whispered, pointing out the window.

The chipmunks had left the windowsill. The squirrels were perking up. The cats stretched their backs; the mutts had started sniffing around the yard. The basset hound still looked mournful—but then, he *was* a basset hound. He hitched up his hind leg and scratched a flea.

Everything wasn't instantly better, but Bax's dad felt relieved, and so the animals felt relieved.

It was a start.

16

First thing Monday morning, Bax, his dad, his mom, Nurse Riley, Coach, and Ms. Starr all met in Principal Gonzalez's office. Nory slipped into the room just as their meeting started, and Ms. Starr turned to Bax and explained that she'd asked her to join them.

"*If* that's all right with you," Ms. Starr said.

"Sure, I guess," Bax said. Nory shrugged at him, and he shrugged back.

"It's my fault for giving Bax so much Burtlebox," Nurse Riley said, picking up where he'd left off.

"No, it's not," Bax's dad said. "What choice did you have?"

"You couldn't have known," Bax's mother said. "We couldn't have known. The doctor prescribed it. They're working on a new potion for Bax now."

"We are all in new territory," Principal Gonzalez said. "But we can learn from this, and the school will make it our mission to support Bax in every way we can."

Ms. Starr smiled at Bax. "Coach and I will work together to help Bax gain control of his fluxing—"

"And now that he's learned how to keep his human mind, it won't be long until he can flux back on his own," Coach said. He rubbed his hands together. "I'm very optimistic. We have the food diary now. We will show it to a nutritionist and learn if any foods are irritating his system, making him flux involuntarily. The doctor can test him for allergies, too. And we can start adding high-nutrient foods to his diet."

"We're sorry this happened," Principal Gonzalez said to Bax's parents. "And we will do everything in our power for it not to happen again."

"This is your team," Coach told Bax. "Right here. Us and your doctors. We have your back."

Bax's mother squeezed his hand. His dad put his arm around his shoulder. Bax felt choked up. All he could do was nod.

Everyone stood up, and the grown-ups shook hands. Coach opened the office door for Bax's mom and filed out behind her.

Nory moved to follow, but Ms. Starr said, "Nory, hold on, please. You too, Bax. Mr. Kapoor, can you stay a little longer?"

Bax's dad looked confused. Ms. Starr closed the office door, and those in the room sat down again.

"What's this about?" Bax's dad asked.

"Bax told me you're an Upside-Down Fuzzy," Ms. Starr said.

"What?" Bax's dad said. He turned red. "I don't . . . I certainly wouldn't—"

"Mr. Kapoor, I think I can help," Ms. Starr said. She gave him a warm smile.

Bax's dad gulped. "And why's that?"

"Because I'm an Upside-Down Fuzzy as well," Ms. Starr answered.

"You are?" Nory exclaimed.

"What?!" Bax had hoped Ms. Starr would be able to do something for his dad, but he hadn't expected this.

Principal Gonzalez templed his fingers. "Eloise is quite extraordinary," he said. "We're extremely lucky to have her."

Eloise, Bax thought. *Eloise Starr, an Upside-Down Fuzzy.* He and Nory shared a marveling look. Ms. Starr had hinted to the class that, like them, her magic was upside down. But she'd never said more than that.

"Can we tell the others?" Nory asked.

"You may," Ms. Starr said. "But do me a favor, please, and don't make a big deal out of it. I don't think it's best if I show my magic during class time. We've all got a lot on our plates right now."

Nory and Bax glanced at each other again. She was right about that.

"As for you, Mr. Kapoor," she went on. "Maybe we could meet sometime and discuss some techniques that might be useful for you?"

Mr. Kapoor's smile was big and wide. "You bet," he said. "I'd like that very much."

When Nory walked into class, she was itching to tell the others what she'd learned about Ms. Starr, who'd stayed behind with Bax and his dad. But the room was already buzzing, and Elliott, Andres, Pepper, and Marigold begged to know everything that had happened at the kittenball game.

Marigold said, "I'm sorry I got angry yesterday. I could have been a lot nicer."

"It's okay," Nory said. "I understand why you didn't want to come to the game." She looked up. "You, too, Andres." He smiled at her, and she turned to Elliott. "It was nice of you to take Andres home."

Elliott nodded. "I couldn't stick with him and stick with you. I didn't know what to do and I— well, I'm sorry I wasn't there to help. It sounds like it was a bit rocky." He grinned, and Nory couldn't help but laugh.

Sebastian was full of news. "The arena got changed back," he told everyone. He was recommitted to his head cone and moved it from side to side so he could see people's faces as he talked. "The game never finished, and the Catnips have to replay the Tidbits this Friday."

"How did they change everything back?" asked Nory.

"Mr. Vitomin and Nurse Riley used a mix of Burtlebox, pomegranate juice, sardine oil, and anti-itch cream, dissolved in almond milk. The same thing they used when the stuff in the lockers turned to stone. But this time, they put it in a high-volume sprayer. It was very cool and it didn't even generate a lot of sound waves," said Sebastian. "I stayed to watch even after my dad came to pick me up. I heard it took most of the weekend to change everything back. People picked up their stuff this morning at the arena. It was all okay, just a little damp and smelled like sardines."

Bax came through the door while everyone was talking. "Excuse me!" he said loudly. "I have something to say."

His gaze met Nory's. The room fell silent.

"It was me," Bax said. "The rocks."

A gasp rippled across the room.

"What the zum-zum?"

"No way."

"Yes," Bax said. "From the very beginning, with the pennies, and then the lockers, and then the arena—it was me."

Bax explained how he hadn't known he was responsible for anything until last night. And he told them about the meeting he'd had that morning. The team, allergy testing, a new potion the doctors wanted to try.

"But I'm really sorry about the rocks." He scuffed the floor with his sneaker. "I made us look bad. The UDM class, I mean. The Sparkies and all those people who signed the petition, they wouldn't have been so upset about the Upside-Down Magic class if it hadn't been for me."

"It was an accident," said Ms. Starr, who had come in behind him. "We all understand that it wasn't on purpose, Bax."

"Are you okay?" Pepper said. "With the Burtlebox side effects and everything?"

"Yeah, are you?" Willa said.

Bax grinned. They cared about him. "Yeah. Nurse Riley and the doctor think there might be other potions they can use, and Coach wants to make me eat a bunch of gross nutritious things after the allergy testing is done. And he says he'll spend extra tutoring hours with me. My mom's excited because Ms. Starr said I should go to yoga with her more often."

"We could keep it a secret," Andres offered. "That it was you who did the rocks."

"No," Bax said. He thought about his dad and all his years of keeping his upside-down magic secret. He thought about Ms. Starr—Ms. *Eloise* Starr—and how she was willing to share *her* secret, even though she was a teacher.

He hitched his shoulders. "You can tell other

people if you want. I am what I am. But I'm going to start a new Pennies for Potions drive, to replace the coins I ruined," he said, holding up a jar of his dad's spare change. "If you want to help, I'll be collecting in the neighborhood after school."

Kittenball practice was that afternoon in the yard. Coach gave them all seaweed and pomegranate juice. Then he got excited about everyone eating kale chips and ran back to his office to get some from his fridge. Nory was alone with Paige, Akari, and Finn.

Nory's mouth was dry. She was nervous. But Bax had been brave enough to tell the UDM kids the truth about the rocks. Nory had to be brave enough to tell the kittenballers about them, too.

Still, it was embarrassing to admit that an upside-down magic kid had caused the trouble. Nory had argued with her teammates until they'd believed her.

Okay. She was going to tell them.

Now.

Okay.

Now, for real.

Paige was fluxing in and out of kitten form. Akari was working on getting his tabby to be orange instead of gray, though right now it was only orange on the left ear. Finn was in kitten form and chasing his tail.

"Guys!" Nory said, still human. "Listen up."

The three kittens lined up in a row and looked at her.

"I was wrong about something," Nory said. "I didn't mean to tell you anything untrue, but I did."

"Mrwow?"

"Pdddp?"

Nory gulped. "The rocks and the lockers? And what happened last night, at the arena? It *was* because of someone in my class."

Paige popped back into human form. Akari and Finn followed.

"You're kidding," Paige said. She put her hands on her hips.

"Seriously?" said Finn. " '*It wasn't us, it wasn't us*,' and now you're admitting it was?"

"They weren't pranks and nothing was on purpose," said Nory. "Someone's magic got messed up with too much of this potion called Burtlebox."

Paige dropped her arms to her sides. She looked willing to listen. Same with Finn and Akari.

So Nory gave them as many details as she could. The only thing she left out was the part about Bax's dad.

"Anyway, Bax is *super* sorry," Nory said.

Paige nodded. "It sounds like it really wasn't his fault."

"Marigold is sorry about shrinking Lacey, too.

And *I'm* sorry about the skunkephant and the mitten."

"Well, like you said, it's not really any worse than a Flare accident or invisible toilets," Akari said. "At camp this summer I turned into a kitten, wrapped myself around my counselor's leg, and bit her ankle."

"I turned into a rat and chewed all my pencils," Paige said.

"I used my dad's closet as a litter box," Finn admitted.

"Who hasn't?" Nory asked.

The others nodded.

"I wish I could say nothing like this will ever happen again," said Nory, "but I don't know if it will or not. Upside-down magic is upside down."

"We're all four of us kittenballers," Paige said. "That's not going to change."

"Yeah," said Akari.

"Finn?" Nory looked at him nervously.

"Okay already," said Finn. "Hey, I've got peanut butter cups. Anyone want candy before Coach gets back?"

"Are you kidding?" Nory said. "Yes!"

The others laughed, and Finn passed out the peanut butter cups, which everyone unwrapped and shoved into their mouths. Nory felt happy and energized and ready to swat the yarnball.

"So what are you guys going to do about the petition?" Paige asked, wiping chocolate off her mouth. "After the rocks on Friday, Lacey went around and got, like, a million signatures. And then a million more this morning."

"Oh," Nory said.

That stupid petition.

She'd thought everything was better. She'd thought everything had been fixed.

But she'd forgotten that petition.

17

Principal Gonzalez called an assembly first thing on Tuesday morning. He announced it over the loudspeaker. He told the teachers to bring their students to the gym.

Ms. Starr asked the UDM students to breathe deep and stay strong. "I don't know what he's going to announce," she said, "but we are not ashamed of who we are. We will hold our heads high. Who's taking Andres? Okay, thank you, Pepper. Now everybody do a quick headstand before we go to the gym."

Nory was nervous. She could tell Bax was

nervous, too, by the way he kept twirling his pencil in his fingers. The students were quiet as they filed out of the classroom.

Except Willa. And Elliott. Because they weren't there.

Where *were* they?

Why were they never where they were supposed to be? Nory couldn't believe Elliott was still keeping secrets.

"Students of Dunwiddle Magic School!" Principal Gonzalez boomed from the platform in the gym. "We have all had an unusual couple of weeks."

Nory's skin got clammy. If the UDM program was going to get canceled, what would they do? Would they all be separated? Where would she go to school?

At the podium, Principal Gonzalez coughed. "Due to the nature of recent events, a petition was created by students and signed by many peo-

ple. It was left on my desk yesterday afternoon."
He held up the petition.

"Those who signed it feel that the magic of
the upside-down students poses a danger. They
feel that danger is worse than the dangers of
Flare magic, fluxed carnivores, Flicker invisibility pranks, and objects dropped by Flyers. The
people who signed the petition wish for the
Upside-Down Magic program to be shut down,
and the students within it to be moved to other
schools, starting next Monday."

"No!" Nory whispered.

Pepper reached over and squeezed her hand.

"To the students who put together the petition, I would like to say that I admire your effort,"
the principal continued. "If there's something
you care about, and you voice your opinion
respectfully, then I will extend the same cour-
tesy by listening to what you have to say."

"We got fifty signatures," said Lacey Clench.

"That means you have to do what we wrote."

He held the petition high. "I am sorry, Miss Clench, but it does not mean that at all."

He ripped the petition straight down the middle.

"It is *not* for students to decide the worthiness—or unworthiness—of their classmates. We at Dunwiddle believe that an Upside-Down Magic program is an asset to everyone. It is not any more dangerous than other daily magical accidents. When I was your age, I made my chair invisible. It was all very funny until my classmate tripped over it and broke his nose. True story."

He waited for the laughter to stop and went on. "I also made countless things invisible that my parents never found, including car keys, the lawn mower, and once, for a terrifying five hours, my little brother." He took a deep breath. "My point is that the Upside-Down Magic program encourages all of us to embrace and understand difference. Loyalty to your school means loyalty to every member of our community. Upside-Down Magic will stay."

Many of the kids cheered and clapped and stomped their feet. As they did, more joined them.

"We're still here!" Nory cried. She turned to Bax and shook him back and forth. "Bax! Bax! The petition didn't work!"

"I know," Bax said with a grin. "I heard."

"I trust we will move on in a spirit of good fellowship," Principal Gonzalez said. "And now, I turn the stage over to Carmen Padillo from the eighth grade, for an announcement." He gestured at the microphone. "Carmen?"

He stepped down from the podium, and Andres's sister, Carmen, stepped up. She wore a jacket and had her hair neatly pulled back. She carried a clipboard and looked like she was ready to give a speech.

Nory saw Elliott and Willa take their seats in the gym. Both were smiling like idiots.

What are they up to? Nory wondered.

Carmen leaned toward the microphone. "On behalf of the eighth grade, and with special thanks to two members of the UDM class, I would like to say—"

She paused dramatically, and the eighth graders finished her sentence with one voice. "PRANK!"

A crew of students rushed onto the platform at the front of the gym, pushing wheelbarrows full of snowballs. They wore gloves and parkas. They picked up the snowballs and pelted the audience.

"Eeek!"

"Pow!"

"My hair!"

"It's cold!"

Elliott ran over to Nory and told her, "We

212

made the snowballs! Me and Willa!"

"You did?"

"That was why I kept going to school early without you! Carmen saw us at our first tutoring session. Ms. Cruciferous was helping Willa do indoor rain in just one tiny part of the room instead of the whole thing, and I was turning it into snow as it came down. Carmen saw us, and got the idea that with our unusual magic, we could help do a prank that was different from any eighth-grade prank in the history of Dunwiddle!"

"We've been making snowballs all week and keeping them in the cafeteria freezer," said Willa.

"Why didn't you tell me?" Nory said.

"Der. Because it was a secret," said Elliott.

"But I—I thought you were—I don't know," said Nory. "I felt really left out, is all."

Elliott's eyes widened. Nory knew that *he* knew how it felt to be left out. "I'm sorry," he said. "I should have told you."

"It's okay," Nory said, and realized it was true. "You couldn't reveal the eighth-grade prank."

"Yeah. But I probably could have kept the secret without making you feel bad," said Elliott. "If I had just thought about it a little more."

Bam! A snowball hit Elliott in the ear.

Nory picked it off the floor, repacked it, and flung it at Pepper.

Elliott beamed.

Pepper dumped snow down the back of Nory's shirt.

Bax combined several snowballs into one giant one and wound his arm in circles, like a baseball player. He seemed to be aiming carefully. Nory stood on her tiptoes in order to follow his gaze.

Bax's snowball arced high and true and hit Lacey Clench with an icy *thwunk*. Lacey squealed and jumped to her feet, brushing snow from her shirt.

"Bax!" Nory cried, delighted.

"What? You think I did that on *purpose*?" he said.

Nory's smile wavered. "You didn't?"

"Are you kidding? I would never. My arm did it. My arm is out of control!"

Bax threw his next one at Coach, who bellowed and pelted another right back at Bax.

Nory soaked it in.

The Upside-Down Magic class was here to stay. She and her friends would continue figuring out their magic. Sometimes they'd succeed and sometimes they'd mess up. Sometimes, unfortunately, they'd do interpretive dance.

She couldn't wait to see what the future would bring.

Acknowledgements

Big thanks and a slurpy squippy kiss to the team at Scholastic, including but not limited to: David Levithan, Jennifer Abbots, Tracy van Straaten, Kelly Ashton, Whitney Steller, Bess Braswell, Rebekah Wallin, Robin Hoffman, Lizette Serrano, Aimee Friedman, and Antonio Gonzalez. Also thanks and a sticky squippy hug to Laura Dail, Tamar Rydzinski, Barry Goldblatt, Tricia Ready, Elisabeth Kaplan, Brian McGuffog, Lauren Kisilevsky (and all the people at Disney we don't know yet!), Eddie Gamarra, Lauren Walters, and Deb Shapiro.

About the Authors

SARAH MLYNOWSKI is the author of many books for tweens, teens, and adults, including the *New York Times* bestselling Whatever After series, the Magic in Manhattan series, and *Gimme a Call*. She would like to be a Flicker so she could make the mess in her room invisible. Visit her online at www.sarahm.com.

LAUREN MYRACLE is the *New York Times* bestselling author of many books for young readers, including The Winnie Years (which begins with *Ten*), the Flower Power series (which begins with *Luv Ya Bunches*), and the Life of Ty series.

She would like to be a Fuzzy so she could talk to unicorns and feed them berries. You can find Lauren online at www.laurenmyracle.com.

EMILY JENKINS is the author of many chapter books, including the Toys Trilogy (which begins with *Toys Go Out*) and the Invisible Inkling series. Her picture books include *Lemonade in Winter, Toys Meet Snow,* and *The Fun Book of Scary Stuff.* She would like to be a Flare and work as a pastry chef. Visit Emily at www.emilyjenkins.com.

Don't miss

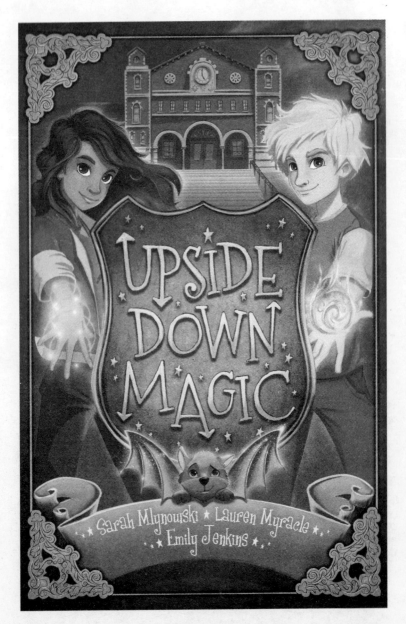

UPSIDE DOWN MAGIC

Sarah Mlynowski ★ Lauren Myracle
★ Emily Jenkins ★